Revenge on Eagle Island

CROSSWAY BOOKS BY STEPHEN BLY

THE STUART BRANNON WESTERN SERIES

Hard Winter at Broken Arrow Crossing
False Claims at the Little Stephen Mine
Last Hanging at Paradise Meadow
Standoff at Sunrise Creek
Final Justice at Adobe Wells
Son of an Arizona Legend

THE NATHAN T. RIGGINS WESTERN
ADVENTURE SERIES
(Ages 9–14)

The Dog Who Would Not Smile
Coyote True
You Can Always Trust a Spotted Horse
The Last Stubborn Buffalo in Nevada
Never Dance with a Bobcat
Hawks Don't Say Goodbye

THE CODE OF THE WEST SERIES

It's Your Misfortune & None of My Own
One Went to Denver & the Other Went Wrong
Where the Deer & the Antelope Play
Stay Away From That City . . . They Call It Cheyenne
My Foot's in the Stirrup . . . My Pony Won't Stand

THE AUSTIN-STONER FILES

The Lost Manuscript of Martin Taylor Harrison
The Final Chapter of Chance McCall
The Kill Fee of Cindy LaCoste

THE LEWIS AND CLARK SQUAD ADVENTURE SERIES
(Ages 9–14)

Intrigue at the Rafter B Ranch
The Secret of the Old Rifle
Treachery at the River Canyon
Revenge on Eagle Island
Danger at Deception Pass
Hazards of the Half-Court Press

LEWIS and CLARK
SQUAD
BOOK FOUR

Revenge on
Eagle Island

STEPHEN BLY

CROSSWAY BOOKS • WHEATON, ILLINOIS
A DIVISION OF GOOD NEWS PUBLISHERS

Revenge on Eagle Island

Copyright © 1998 by Stephen Bly

Published by Crossway Books
       a division of Good News Publishers
       1300 Crescent Street
       Wheaton, Illinois 60187

Cover illustration: Sergio Giovine

Cover design: Cindy Kiple

First printing, 1998

Printed in the United States of America

Library of Congress Cataloging-in-Publication Data
Bly, Stephen, 1944-
    Revenge on Eagle Island / Stephen Bly.
        p.   cm.—(The Lewis & Clark Squad adventure series ; bk. 4)
    Summary: When the basketball squad travels to Flathead Lake, Montana, to attend an Indian powwow and play in a tournament, they learn a lesson about trading revenge for forgiveness.
    ISBN 0-89107-984-X
    [1. Basketball—Fiction. 2. Revenge—Fiction. 3. Christian life—Fiction. 4. Mystery and detective stories.]   I. Title.
II. Series: Bly, Stephen A., 1944-   Lewis & Clark Squad adventure series ; bk. 4.
PZ7.B6275Re 1998
[Fic]—dc21   97-32232

06		05		04		03		02		01		00		99		98
15	14	13	12	11	10	9	8	7	6	5	4	3	2	1

For my good pal
Mitchell Pentzer

One

*N*ever before had Cody Clark seen Larry Lewis hurdle a three-foot-tall pyramid of Quaker State 10-30 Motor Oil quart containers. In fact, he had never seen anyone on earth leap over a stack of motor oil and blast through the doorway of a Montana minimart while screaming "NO!" at the top of his lungs. Cody dropped the package of old-fashioned doughnuts back onto the shelf and jogged out after his shaggy-haired friend.

"Larry? Hey . . . what's happening?"

Jeremiah Yellowboy puffed out into the bright sunlight behind his two friends. "What's Larry screaming about?"

"I don't know." Cody ran toward the pickup camper parked by pump number 8. "Larry, what's wrong?"

Rage flashed across Larry's slightly tanned face. "They took it!"

Cody rocked forward on the toes of his brown cowboy boots and peered into the pickup window. "Who took it?"

Jeremiah shoved his way between them. "What did they take?"

Suddenly Larry sprinted toward Missoula's busy Brooks Boulevard. "There they are! Stop them! Call the cops! Give it back!" His screams were drowned out by the noise of the traffic.

Only a step or two behind him, Cody hollered, "What did they take?"

"The kid in the Orlando Magic hat stole my basketball! I saw him lift it right out of the front seat of the rig while I was in the store!"

"Where is he?"

"In the red Dakota pickup pulling the trailer with jet skis. I've got to stop him!"

Larry darted into the traffic, but Cody and Jeremiah grabbed his arms and yanked him back to the sidewalk just as a logging truck roared by with air horn blasting.

"Let me go!" Larry screamed. "They're getting away!"

"It's only a basketball," Cody reminded him. "It's not worth getting run over by a truck."

Jeremiah wrapped his arm around Larry's shoulder. "Listen, Capt. Lewis, you brought two basketballs, right?"

Larry was almost in tears. "But he stole my auto-graphed ball!"

"You brought an autographed basketball on a camp-ing trip?" Cody quizzed.

"Whose autograph?" Jeremiah let his arm drop to his side.

"Mine."

"What?"

"It says 'LBL-NBA MVP-2007' and then has my autograph. When I get that NBA Most Valuable Player award in '07, I want to look back and point to that ball."

"Why don't you write that on one of your other basketballs?" Cody advised. They stood on the chipped concrete sidewalk as the Friday afternoon traffic whizzed by.

"But that was my ball. He shouldn't have taken it. Now my whole weekend, my whole summer, my life is ruined!"

"Hey, when things go bad for me, I just down a twenty-ounce Mountain Dew and a box of Twinkies," Jeremiah confided.

"Townie has the right idea. True champions always have setbacks, but you can't let that throw you off," Cody advised.

"As MJ would say, 'Twenty-six times my team's counted on me making the game winning shot, and I've missed, and that is why I succeed,'" Jeremiah mimicked.

"Yeah, champions thrive on adversity," Cody added.

Larry sulked along one step ahead of them. "You guys are right. I'm too good a basketball player to let this ruin a tournament. Me and Michael Jordan do have a lot in common."

Cody glanced over at Jeremiah, who rolled his eyes toward the sky. Larry headed for the camper.

"Aren't you going to buy something to drink?" Jeremiah called out.

"Yeah, I'll be right there. I'm going to get my game ball. I'm not about to let that baby out of my sight."

Cody and Jeremiah strolled toward the front door of the minimart and met Feather as she exited the ladies' room.

"You missed all the excitement," Cody announced as he held the front door open for her.

"What excitement? And I'm quite capable of opening my own doors."

"I was, eh, holding this open for Townie."

"What excitement?" she demanded.

"Oh, the pride of Indiana just had a basketball stolen, and then a logging truck almost ended his short but colorful basketball career."

"I missed all of that?"

"Every minute is an exciting adventure with the Lewis and Clark Squad," Cody teased.

"Really? Being stuck in the back of that camper with you three for 110 miles of winding Highway 12 was extremely boring," she countered.

"Oh . . . those minutes. Well," Cody offered, "you could have played Risk with us."

"Conquering the entire known world is not exactly my idea of a fun way to spend time."

"You're kidding me, right?"

The freckles across Feather's face seemed to underline the glare in her eyes, and Cody sheepishly followed her into the minimart.

Larry Bird Lewis climbed out of the back of the pickup-mounted camper and stared across Flathead Lake. His blond hair was tousled and uncombed after the six-hour ride from Halt, Idaho, to Elmo, Montana. He tried to tuck his white and red University of Indiana tank top into his red shorts with his left hand. His right hand cradled a synthetic leather basketball that had the freshly lettered words: "LBL—NBA MVP—2007 #2."

"Where's the gym?" he queried. "I don't see a gym, Jeremiah."

Cody Clark's cowboy hat was pushed to the back of his head. The heels of his boots hit the dry, dusty soil of the hillside-turned-temporary-campground. He could feel the sweat-soaked sleeveless black T-shirt sticking to his back. His jeans felt stiff. He uncoiled the dirt-colored stiff nylon rope in his hand and began to build a loop. "Gym? We're camping out. Remember?"

Larry tried to dribble the ball on the dirt, but it hit a rock and began to pick up speed as it rolled down the hill. Cody quickly roped the ball, and Larry ran to retrieve it. "Yeah, but we're having a basketball tournament. Do we go back to that town on the south of the lake—what was it called?"

"Polson?" Cody offered, as he stepped aside to let Feather climb down behind him.

"Yeah, Polson. Do we go in there to play in the tournament? Where are we going to practice anyway? I have our practice schedules made out for the entire weekend. We won't be able to shoot around very good with only one basketball. I can't believe that stupid kid stole my other ball! Man, am I going to get even with him!"

"Don't get carried away with revenge," Cody cautioned.

"Oh, I'll be fair," Larry insisted. "I was only thinking of tying him to a wagon wheel and burning his flesh off."

Cody pulled off his hat and ran his fingers through his hair. *Lord, I think Larry's getting a little carried away.*

Feather Trailer-Hobbs lifted her waist-long brown pony-tail and let the warm July breeze cool the back of her neck. Her tie-dyed T-shirt was knotted just above the waist of her cut-off jeans shorts. "I thought there would be more tepees! It's mainly all campers, trailers, and travel homes."

"The tepees will be raised this evening," Jeremiah Yellowboy called out as he strolled around to the back of the rig. "Hey, you guys want a Mountain Dew? I think I'll have another. Man, it's hot, isn't it?" His Chicago Bulls cap was set bill-back on his head, and sweat trickled through the black butch haircut.

"Where do we play basketball?" Larry asked again.

"Probably down there." Jeremiah pointed back toward the paved highway.

"Outside?" Larry gasped.

"This is a powwow, not the NCAA play-offs!" Feather put in.

"Do we play on concrete or asphalt courts?" Larry pressed.

"Dirt, rock, and grass," Jeremiah informed him.

"You're kidding me. I didn't bring my dirt tennis shoes. I thought we'd be in a gym."

"Whatever gave you that idea?" Cody asked.

Feather shaded her eyes and searched the dusty field below them. "It will be just like when we practice out at Cody's barn. I mean, without the dried manure."

"But this is a tournament. Surely they have something better."

"It's not a tournament. It's a powwow." Jeremiah waved to people pulling up in a blue Ford pickup and camper. Then he turned to Larry. "Basketball is just one of the recreation activities."

Cody glanced over at Jeremiah. "Townie, who's that you waved at in the silver rig?"

"That's my Aunt Lucy."

"Did she bring Honey?" Cody gasped.

"Yep. Now don't act like a fool in front of her," Jeremiah teased.

Feather squinted her eyes and stared toward the camper with the worn off-white paint. "The totally awesome Miss Honey Del Mateo? I'll finally get to meet her? What does she look like?"

"Actually, I haven't seen her in a few years," Cody explained. "I don't know if I'd recognize . . ."

When his eyes met the deep brown eyes of the black-haired, dark-skinned girl, he stood tall, straightened his cowboy hat, and let his sentence fade into the short, dry grass of the Montana hillside.

"Hi, Cody!"

Some songs touch off a flood of memories. The mind races back to a particular scene . . . once again to thrill . . . or terrify. Honey's voice was like a pleasant song to Cody, like a wonderful mild spring wind on a blue-sky day. There was a tickle in his throat, a leap in his spirit, and a dizziness in his mind.

"Cody?" the thirteen-year-old girl repeated.

"Oh! Yeah . . . hi!" Then he blushed and turned to Feather and Larry. "Eh, this is my Honey!"

"That I can see!" Feather mumbled.

"No, I mean . . . not my honey . . . but my friend Honey Del Mateo. Honey, this is Leather and Farry."

"Who?"

"I mean Feather and Larry!" *I'm goin' to die. Clark, you are an idiot. Why did I ever come here? It was Townie's idea. I didn't want to do this!*

"Feather? That's a wonderful name." Honey smiled.

"Thanks. My mother says the trees named me."

The girl with the turquoise and silver necklace and the scoop-necked pink T-shirt scooted over to Feather. "That's cool. My grandma named me."

"Really?"

"Yeah, her name was Bea. And she named my sister Blossom and me Honey."

"Wow, I like that. Cody thinks my name's weird."

"I never said it was weird."

"But I can tell what you think, Cody Wayne Clark!" Feather spun on the heels of her knee-high moccasins and looked Honey in the eyes. "Did you know that Cody has had a crush on you ever since you kissed him in the first grade?"

Cody felt the blood rush from his face. *No! She didn't really say that! I'm goin' to die! Lord, if You wanted to open the earth and swallow me up, that would be all right with me.*

Honey leaned her face only inches from Feather's. "You're kidding me, right?"

"Nope. Am I right, Townie?" Feather pressed.

"Don't sucker me into this." Jeremiah grinned from ear to ear. "I'm goin' for a hike. You guys want to go for a hike?"

"Sure." Feather beamed.

"You two can't come," Jeremiah announced.

Feather slammed her thin hands on her hips. "And why not?"

"Because those honey-huts are just for boys. The girls' ones are over there by the cottonwoods!" He waved his hand toward the highway.

Cody, still carrying his rope and a scarlet blush on his tanned face, traipsed after Jeremiah. He thought Larry was following them, but he didn't turn around and look until he heard a basketball dribble on the hillside behind him.

"Hey, guys, catch my ball!" Larry hollered.

Jeremiah jammed his Nike tennis shoe on top of the ball. "Whoa . . . Feather ribbed you pretty good back there," he teased.

Cody heaved a deep sigh. "How long do you think it would take me to hitchhike home?"

"That bad, huh?"

"Have you really had a crush on Honey since the first grade?" Larry asked, retrieving the ball.

Cody glanced up. The swiftly moving scattered clouds stacked up against the towering granite spine of the Rocky Mountains on the east side of Flathead Lake. "Looks like we might have thunder showers before dark," he announced.

"I'll take that for a yes. I can't believe you introduced us as Leather and Farry."

"Yeah, Clark's really a smooth operator, isn't he?" Townie teased. "Girls just fall head over heels when they're around him."

"You mean, they stumble trying to get away," Larry howled.

Townie joined in. "My own opinion is that he spends too much time talkin' to horses."

"Oh, this is great," Cody moaned. "I make a complete fool of myself with Honey, and then you two dis me down here."

"Toughen up, paleface." Jeremiah grinned. "The weekend just began. You'll have to admit, you were pretty dorky."

"But . . . but she's changed!"

"You didn't expect her to look like a first grader still, did you?"

"No, but I didn't know she'd look like a Native American LeAnn Rimes either."

"Who?" Larry asked.

"Never mind." Jeremiah chuckled and handed his empty Mountain Dew can to Larry.

"What am I supposed to do with this?"

Jeremiah pulled open the aluminum and fiberglass door of the portable potty. "Recycle it." Then he slammed the door behind him.

Cody and Larry watched as pickups, campers, and cars pulled onto the grassy hillside.

"I should have gotten a better tan." Larry glanced down at his pale arms. "Are we the only white kids here?"

"I doubt that. It doesn't matter, does it?"

"I hope not, but I'm beginning to know what General Custer must have felt like," Larry mumbled.

"Colonel Custer."

"Really?"

"Lieutenant Colonel George Armstrong Custer," Cody informed him. "He was blond-headed like you."

"That's an encouraging thought."

"No worry. Custer was from Ohio, not Indiana," Cody needled.

"Hey, did I see Yellowboy go in there?" The booming voice caused both boys to spin around.

Cody stared as a six-foot-tall, two-hundred-pound boy with long black braids strutted toward them.

"You mean Townie?"

The towering boy leaned closer to Cody and Larry. "Who's Townie?"

"Downtown Jeremiah Yellowboy."

The boy pointed a massive, callused right hand at the closed green door. "He's in there?"

"Yeah. Do you know him?"

The boy stepped over to the portable restroom, gripped the side of it, and began to rock it back and forth.

"Hey!" Jeremiah screamed. "Cut that out, Clark! I mean it!"

"It's not me," Cody yelled. Then he turned to the big boy who wore only jeans, thongs, and a brown leather vest.

"I said stop it!" Jeremiah continued to yell. "This is definitely not funny!"

"Don't do that!" Cody grabbed the boy's thick, muscled arm.

"Who are you?"

"I'm Jeremiah's friend."

"Well, I'm his cousin!"

"Eddie, is that you?" Jeremiah yelled.

"It ain't Joe Buffalo!" The big boy backed away from the portable outhouse. "Who are these vanilla-colored friends of yours?"

A disheveled Jeremiah Yellowboy staggered out the door into the bright sunshine of the late July afternoon. "Eddie!" Townie slapped high fives with the larger boy. "Grandpa didn't say anything about you guys coming!"

"Dad just decided yesterday morning."

"Eddie, these are my friends Cody and Larry."

"You must be Cody." He nodded.

"How could you tell?" Cody questioned.

"The cowboy hat, boots, and rope. Every cowboy in Montana is named Cody, Ty, or Clay."

"I'm from Idaho."

"Whatever."

"Guys, this is my cousin Eddie Winterhawk."

"Are you related to everybody in the West?" Larry pressed.

"Only the bronzed ones! Me and Eddie were born on the same day."

"But I'm older," Winterhawk bragged.

"That's obvious." Larry shrugged.

"Only by six hours."

"Are you kidding?" Larry mumbled. "You're only thirteen?"

"Twelve. Me and Yellowboy won't be thirteen until next month."

"Do you play basketball?"

"Do Apps have spots?" The big boy turned back to Jeremiah. "Did you get your feather yet?"

"Nah. All I've got is a hawk feather. How about you?"

"I've got a great horned owl, but not an eagle. I'm third on the list next time a BLM guy finds a dead one. You're going to get your new name on Sunday night, aren't you?"

"Yeah, but Grandpa said I can use one of his feathers if I want to."

"Yeah," Eddie added. "I guess I'll have to do that, too."

"Come on over and see my new buckskin outfit that Mom made," Eddie insisted. "It is totally awesome. I can hardly wait to play the drums."

Jeremiah turned to Larry and Cody. "When Eddie plays the drums, you can hear them for five miles."

"Somehow that doesn't surprise me," Larry mumbled to Cody.

Jeremiah started to tramp off alongside his cousin. Then he turned back. "Hey, you guys want to come along?"

"Nah. I think I'll go back up to the camper," Larry replied.

"Yeah," Cody began, "I'll go back . . ." *The camper? That's where Honey is! I can't go back there . . . ever! Oh, man, this is a lousy weekend, and it's only Friday night.*

"Well, tell Grandpa I'm at Eddie's."

Cody stood motionless as Jeremiah and his cousin strolled toward a long travel home with Washington license plates. Larry plodded up the hill.

Lord, I don't like being embarrassed. I just want to hide

over in the corner and watch the others. Why can't I just go through life unnoticed?

"Are you in line?"

Cody whipped around to see a brown-skinned five-year-old boy wearing only a pair of jeans hop from one dusty foot to the other.

"Eh . . . no."

"Good!" the boy shouted and plunged into the portable outhouse.

By the time Cody reached the tepee, Larry was stretched out in a plastic chaise lounge with a Mountain Dew in one hand and his basketball in the other.

"Where are the girls?"

"They went over to Honey's camper to tell secrets about Cody Wayne Clark."

"Really?"

"How would I know? Cody, my man, you need to chill off. You're stumbling around like a nerd with a new web site."

"I am not!"

"You are too!"

"Feather embarrassed me."

"Embarrassed you? I'll tell you what's going to be embarrassing—playing Eddie Winterhawk. You guard him. The guy's a mountain. His neck is bigger than my waist. There is no way that guy is twelve! I wonder if I could hire him to pound the kid who stole my ball?"

Cody pulled a Coke from the dark blue ice chest and plopped down on the dry grass next to Larry. "With any luck we'll be eliminated before we have to play Eddie's team."

"I didn't travel to the edge of the earth to be eliminated!" Larry yapped.

"This isn't the edge of the earth," Cody insisted. "See those mountains over there?"

"Yeah."

"That's the edge of the earth."

Cody and Larry stared silently across the vast lake. The clouds that were white and puffy as they sailed over Flathead Lake looked dark and threatening stacked up against the treeless granite peaks of the Rocky Mountains. Cody could smell a hint of sulphur in the hot, dry July air.

"When do things get started?" Larry finally asked.

"The Grand Entry begins about 8:00 P.M."

"Is that where Townie gets to wear the beaded jacket that Mr. Levine gave him?"

"Everyone will be dressed up. It's really cool."

"When will Townie dance?"

"I don't know which dances come first."

"What do you mean, which dances?"

"They have Men's Traditional, Men's Fancy, Women's Traditional Buckskin, Jingle Dress Dance, and Men's Grass Dance."

"Whoa! You're kidding me! I thought they just hopped around while someone beat boom, boom, boom on the drum."

"You're in for an education, Mr. Lewis."

"And so are you, Mr. Clark. Here comes Feather, and she looks happier than a Hoosier with a hoop."

Cody refused to look toward the Del Mateo camper. "Is Honey with her?"

"Nope."

Cody doodled in the dirt next to where he was sitting.

"I know a lot of secrets, Mr. Cody Wayne Clark," Feather boasted as she came up.

"Like what?" Larry asked.

"Like the fact that Cody used to write mushy love notes to Honey Del Mateo."

"I did not."

"You did so."

"I was in the first grade," Cody boomed. "You don't write mushy love notes in the first grade! You can hardly write your name."

"She still has them."

"Really?" Larry questioned.

"In a shoe box back home. And Cody asked her to marry him," Feather teased.

"I was only six! It doesn't count!"

Larry took a deep swig of his soda and then sat up in the chaise lounge. "Well, did she accept?"

"She told him she'd think about it."

"You were quite a romeo, Clark!" Larry chided.

"I wonder whatever happened to those qualities?" Feather mused.

"Burned out young, I suppose." Larry began to giggle.

"All right! If you two are finished . . ."

"Finished?" Feather smirked. "I've just gotten started.

I know some other secrets. Honey plays the flute when Jeremiah dances."

"I know that," Cody maintained.

"I'll bet you didn't know that Honey's going with a guy who's almost fifteen, named Daniel Old Horn."

Two

✺

*W*ith his sweat-soaked sleeveless black T-shirt in his right hand and his black beaver felt cowboy hat in his left, Cody collapsed on the braided rug stretched across the dirt floor of the tepee. The rug felt rough on his bare back, but it was cooler than wearing the shirt. Larry had already crumpled down beside him when Jeremiah Yellowboy slumped through the open canvas doorway and handed them both a Mountain Dew.

"Setting up a tepee is hard work!" Larry groaned.

"Yeah." Jeremiah held the cold can to his forehead. "In the old days the women always set up the tepee."

"Sounds good to me. Where were Feather and Honey when we needed them?" Larry tipped his green can back and guzzled a third of it in one swallow.

Cody began to tug off his cowboy boots. "Honey said she wanted Feather to meet some of her friends."

"How many friends does Honey have?" Larry asked.

"She knows everyone." Jeremiah lay back with his

head on a rolled-up sleeping bag. "Honey's never been a shy person."

"You mean Clark might not be the only boy she kissed in the first grade?"

"I can't answer that—at least, not if I want to live another day!" He laughed.

Cody sat up and took another swig from his soda. "Look . . . let's have an understanding. The first grade was a long time ago, and I won't bring up what happened to you guys in the first grade, and don't you bring up what happened to me."

"Whoa, secrets!" Larry grinned. "I spent the first grade in Indiana, and the only thing of significance I can remember was that was the year I made my first legitimate free throw. So just what exactly happened to Mr. Jeremiah Yellowboy when he was six?"

"Cody Wayne Clark, you say one word about that, and the Battle of the Little Big Horn will look like a church picnic in comparison!"

"All right!" Larry laughed. "This must really be good. What did Townie do?"

Cody lay back down on the braided rug and closed his eyes. "In the interest of racial harmony and in order to avoid the needless shedding of blood—namely my own—I think I'll decline to comment on that."

"Smart move," Jeremiah declared.

"I think you chickened out," Larry protested.

"There's an old saying out west," Cody went on. "When surrounded by Indians, stick a feather in your hair and dance."

"I never heard that one," Jeremiah hooted.

"I just made it up."

"Speaking of feathers," Larry put in, "what's this deal about you and Eddie needing eagle feathers?"

"Oh, it's something that we do when we get our names." Jeremiah crawled over on his hands and knees and began digging through a brown paper grocery sack. "Have you guys seen the Oreos?"

"You finished them back at Ravalli."

"Oh, man, really? Hey, here are some oatmeal raisin cookies! You guys want some?"

"I don't like raisins," Larry replied.

"Me either," Cody chimed in.

"Hey, that's cool! I'll have them all to myself." Jeremiah dragged the sack of cookies back over to his sleeping bag armrest. "Anyway, when the elders give us our names, we are supposed to wear an eagle feather in a headband. But since it's illegal to shoot them, eagle feathers are tough to come by. Either you buy one from a poacher, which could get you arrested, or wait for a BLM or BIA or forestry guy to find a dead one. They bring the carcass to the tribe so we can have the body parts."

"Body parts? Yuuck!" Larry groaned. "Will they let you substitute other feathers?"

"Oh, we can use hawk, osprey, or owl, but everyone knows that eagle feathers are best."

Cody sat up and rubbed his arms. "Hey, I saw a movie on TV one time where a kid snuck up in the rocks into an eagle nest, hid under the sticks, grabbed the eagle's legs when it landed, then jerked out a tail feather with his teeth, and let the eagle go."

"Yeah . . . right." Jeremiah shrugged. "Those kinds of things happen only in movies."

"I wonder if eagles lose feathers? You know, a lot of birds have a few feathers fall out around their nests," Cody pondered.

"Hey," Larry shouted, "let's go find an eagle nest!"

Cody glanced at Jeremiah and then back at Larry. "Do you know what an eagle nest looks like?"

Larry shook his head. "I don't even know what an eagle looks like. They have white heads, don't they?"

"It doesn't matter." Jeremiah shrugged. "They usually nest in rocks, cliffs, or tall trees—none of which are around here. I guess I'll just wear one of my grandfather's eagle feathers."

"What's wrong with your hawk feather?" Larry asked.

"Well, I'll be dancing to the eagle song. It's not exactly proper to wear hawk feathers while dancing to the eagle song."

Larry shook his head. "This whole powwow thing is a lot more complicated than I thought."

"Hey, you guys want next?" The high-pitched girl's voice brought all three boys to a sitting position.

Cody scrambled to pull on his wet T-shirt. "Feather, you can't come in here! I'm not dressed!"

Honey stuck her head in next to Feather's. "He's really shy, isn't he? As if we've never seen a boy with his shirt off!"

Feather mumbled, "Eh, I haven't . . ."

"You're kidding me!" Honey squealed.

"No, really . . . I mean, not up close."

"Where've you been, Feather-girl? Living in a cave?"

"No. In a tepee."

"You live in a tepee?"

"Until last week when me and Mom moved to town."

Honey crossed her arms and shook her head. "Well . . . anyway they have the baskets set up, and we reserved one. You three want to play us a game?"

Larry leaped to his feet. "Who's standing who?"

"Me, Honey, and Daniel will take on you three," Feather challenged.

"Daniel?" Cody asked.

"Daniel Old Horn. I mentioned him, didn't I?"

The portable baskets were first rate, with glass backboards and breakaway rims. Beyond that, there was little resemblance to a basketball court. Even on the flattest area near the portable outhouses, the hillside sloped away from the basket and sideways toward the highway. The dirt was fairly hard-packed, fairly clear of grass, and partially cleared of rocks. Dribbling was an adventure. The ball seldom bounced straight up and sometimes didn't bounce at all. Then unexpectedly it would hit a rock and squirt out to the side, far from the dribbler's grasp.

Danny Old Horn was Cody's height but had broader shoulders. His black hair hung, unbraided, well past his shoulders. He had a permanent smile that revealed straight white teeth but absolutely nothing about what he was thinking.

Cody looked him over as all six shot around in the now slightly cloudy but muggy late afternoon.

Lord, I don't know why I'm jealous of Danny. I mean, Honey's not my girlfriend or anything. It's just . . . well, for two weeks I've been looking forward to seeing her, and now . . .

This is stupid, Lord. Why do I always act so dumb around girls?

Except for Feather.

She's different.

Larry pulled Jeremiah and Cody to the side of the dirt court. "Who's guarding who?"

"I think Cody ought to take Daniel," Jeremiah suggested. "They are about the same size."

"Okay." Larry nodded. "And I'll guard Feather."

"Oh no, I'm not guarding Honey. She'll complain to Grandpa about every bump and push."

"I'll guard Honey," Cody offered.

Both boys stared at him.

"Not quite." Larry grinned. "It's too hard to dribble when your tongue is dragging in the dirt."

"What do you mean by that?"

"What he means is you're not objective enough to guard her. You stick with Danny. I'll take Honey, and Townie can guard Feather."

"Not objective enough? You don't think I can guard a pretty girl?"

Larry nodded his head. "We don't think you can guard Honey."

What they had was Daniel Old Horn's hook shot underneath, Feather's quick defense, and two three-pointers by Honey. When they stopped for a break, the score was fourteen to eight, with all four of their baskets coming from Larry's jump shots over the outstretched arms of Honey Del Mateo.

The three boys shared a plastic bottle of blue Gatorade while Larry drew out a play in the dirt. "Look, we can't catch them unless we can make some threes."

"Feather's in my face. I can't get a shot off," Townie complained.

"Fake a three and drive past her," Larry suggested.

"I can't outrun her, and even if I did, it's only a two-pointer. Besides, good ol' Danny boy will be there to stuff it down my throat."

"No, the minute you fake the three, Cody will run to the top of the key."

"What key?" Cody jibed.

"Well, where the key would be if we had a key. Danny will trail after you. Townie, you take two steps. Danny will drop back. Then you pass to Cody."

"I'm not going to shoot a three," Cody protested.

"Here's the thing. You pass it to me. Then set a pick on Honey, and I break around and take a three-point jump shot from the top of the key."

Jeremiah looked over at Cody. "Where does he come up with all these plays?"

"He lies awake at night."

"What do we do if it works?"

"Run in on the other side until they figure it out. If we can make two or three, we'll catch up with them."

Larry tossed the ball in to Cody, who bounced it over to Jeremiah. He faked a shot. Instead of going for a block, Feather dropped back for a rebound, leaving Townie open. He shrugged, then tossed up a shot.

Nothing but net.

He turned to Larry. "Sorry!"

"No *problemo, amigo.*" Larry grinned. "Keep draining those if you get an opening."

Feather bounced the ball into Honey, who made a no-look pass to Danny. He drove to the basket. The whole play was so quick and slick that Cody didn't have time to move. Danny crashed into him and missed the lay-in.

"Offensive foul!" Larry hollered.

"Foul?" Danny shook his head. "We barely bumped." He reached down and pulled Cody to his feet.

"Well, it's our ball. It didn't touch anything before it rolled out of bounds," Larry insisted.

"I won't argue with that." Danny scooted over to guard Cody.

This time they ran Larry's play. Jeremiah faked Feather and drove to the basket, then passed off to Cody as Danny dropped back. Cody bounced the ball to Larry and set the pick. Larry dashed around Cody with Honey in quick pursuit. She didn't take her eye off the ball. As a result she crashed into Cody, with both of them tumbling to the dirt.

Larry let out a whoop when his three-pointer banked

into the net, but Cody was trying to catch his breath with Honey sprawled on top of him.

"That looks cozy," Feather mumbled.

"Honey, are you all right?" Danny ran over and helped Del Mateo to her feet. "For Pete's sake, Clark, you didn't have to flatten her!" he growled.

Cody lay in the dirt gasping for air.

"It was a legal pick, and you know it!" Larry protested.

"I'm okay," Honey panted.

Danny slammed his right foot into Cody's heaving chest. "Let me tell you something—you knock Honey to the ground again, and I'll bust your lip. Have you got that?"

In an attempt to catch his breath, Cody shoved Danny's foot off his chest. This surprised Old Horn, and he staggered back, tripped on a rock, and landed on his rear.

With his dark brown eyes flashing, Danny leaped to his feet. "If you want to have it out right now, it's all right with me!" He dove at Cody, who was now propped up on one elbow. Cody rolled over quickly, and Danny crashed into the dirt. Without thinking, Cody pounced on Danny and yanked the boy's right arm behind his back, pinning his face to the dirt.

"Let me up!" Danny screamed.

Cody noticed several older Native American kids starting to gather around them. "Honey, I'm sorry we crashed into the ground. I just tried to screen you off, not have a wreck."

"Hey, it's okay, Cody. I ran into you. I didn't know you were so, eh, well built. You filled out since the first grade."

"Yeah," Cody mumbled, "so have you. . . . I mean . . ." *Oh no. I'm going to die of embarrassment.*

He immediately let loose of Danny's arm and stood up. Jeremiah, Feather, and Larry scooted up by his side. He reached down and offered his hand to Danny, who refused his help.

Danny struggled to his feet and held out his hand to Honey Del Mateo. "Come on, girl. I agreed to play basketball, not football. Let's hike over to the arena and check things out for tonight. Maybe next year Yellowboy will leave his friends at home."

Amid the stares of a dozen brown faces, the Lewis and Clark Squad turned and walked away from the basketball area.

"Well, we've been here an hour, and Cody's got in a fight," Larry prodded. "You're the Dennis Rodman of three-on-three basketball."

"It wasn't Cody's fault," Feather insisted. "It was a good pick."

"Yeah, Cody outplayed him and outwrestled him. Man, I can't believe how quick you pinned Danny," Jeremiah added.

"I've had practice. Remember, I have three older brothers. It's the only way I have a chance against them when we wrestle."

"You've pinned Denver like that?" Feather asked.

"Well, actually it's never worked before. But I've tried."

"Are you okay, partner?" Jeremiah quizzed.

"Once I got my breath back, I was fine."

"Did you lose your breath because of the collision or

just from the shock of having Honey Del Mateo draped all over you?" Feather probed.

"It was Larry's play, and you make it sound like I did it on purpose."

"It wasn't your fault," Jeremiah confirmed. "But Danny's not exactly a forgiving type."

"Well, I'm going into the tepee and not come out until Monday," Cody grumbled.

"Really?" Feather pressed.

"No. But I am going to stay out of sight for a while. I don't intend to tick anyone else off this weekend."

"Don't worry about it," Jeremiah insisted. "You guys have a right to be here. Besides, a little racial harassment builds character."

"Where did you hear that?" Larry asked.

"Cody Wayne Clark told me that one time. Let's go into the tepee and finish our game of Risk," Jeremiah suggested. "I think I know where the other bag of Oreos is."

"I'm going with you," Feather announced. "I don't want to sit in a hot camper all by myself. I'm allowed to go into the tepee, aren't I?"

"Well, yeah, but . . ."

"You aren't going to do some disgusting boy things, are you?"

"Like what?" Larry quizzed.

"Like pulling off your shirts and playing tunes with your armpits."

Cody began to laugh. "Well, we were going to practice a three-part harmony of 'When the Saints Go Marchin' In,' but I suppose we can wait till later."

Larry and Jeremiah doubled up in laughter.

"Hey, hey," Townie guffawed, "I get to play bass this time!"

"You are gross. You are all tasteless, disgusting, and gross!" Feather accused.

"So do you want to come play Risk with us or not?" Cody stood by the open doorway of the off-white canvas tepee.

"Yes, I think I will."

"Really?" Larry gasped.

"What's the matter? Don't you think a girl can rule the world?"

Jeremiah was putting on his beaded buckskin jacket as Cody, Feather, and Larry continued the board game.

"You can't take over a country, declare neutrality, and remove all the armies from it," Larry protested.

"I just did," Feather announced. "South America is now a war-free zone, never again to face needless military destruction."

"That's not the way you play this game!" Cody insisted.

Feather curled a strand of her long brown hair across her top lip like a mustache. "It's called progress. The age of great imperialistic powers is over. Countries can no longer be controlled by the military-industrial complex of a previous generation."

"What did she say?" Jeremiah called out from across the room.

"She said she doesn't like Risk and is never going to ask to play it again," Larry bantered.

"I didn't ask to play this game. Cody invited me. Didn't you, Cody?"

"Eh, yeah. But I assumed we were going to follow the rules."

Feather turned up her slightly freckled nose. "Why did you assume that?"

"Hey, can I come in?"

It was Honey Del Mateo at the open doorway of the tepee. She didn't wait for an answer but skipped over to Jeremiah. "Is that your new coat? Wow, it's really awesome!"

"It's an original," Townie boasted. "Did Grandpa tell you how I got it?"

"He said that you guys helped capture some drug runners, and an old man gave it to you as a reward."

"Well, it wasn't all that dramatic," Jeremiah began.

"It was to me!" Larry chirped. "They had guns and everything."

Honey wandered over to the three playing the board game. "Who's winning?"

"Eh . . . we're sort of at a stalemate," Cody reported. "Feather occupied all the countries between me and Larry and declared them neutral. So we don't have anyone left to attack."

"Wow, that's cool!"

"It's not in the rules!" Larry moaned.

"You've got them squealing. That means you must be winning, Feather."

"She is not winning; she's cheating!" Larry protested.

"I'm going to go get dressed for the Grand Entry. Can you come help me, Feather?"

"Sure. This game is really boring anyway."

"It's only boring if you don't let the armies attack other countries," Larry complained.

"Hey, Honey," Cody called as the girls reached the doorway.

"Yes, dear?" Feather giggled.

"No, I meant Honey," Cody groaned. He could feel his face flush. "Is Daniel still mad at me?"

"He did mention something about breaking your arm. Or was it your neck?"

"Oh, man. I didn't mean to pin him like that. I just didn't want to fight at all. I don't know why things like this keep happening to me."

Honey turned to Feather. "Does he get into these situations often?"

"Last time it was when he protected my honor."

The girls giggled all the way to the camper.

Cody lay on his back and stared up at the small round opening high at the top of the tepee. *Lord, I don't even want to be here. Everything I do or say either gets me into trouble or embarrasses me to death.*

"Hey, you want to go down to the courts and see if there's an empty basket?" Larry asked.

"Are you kidding?" Cody moaned. "I'm not going down there again."

"You mean, until the tournament tomorrow."

Cody didn't answer.

Larry cleared his throat. "I said—"

"I know what you said, Larry!" Cody huffed.

"Okay, okay, I'm going to go shoot a few hoops. I don't suppose you want to go, do you, Townie?"

"Nah, I've got to go with my grandpa. He wants to show off my new beaded jacket to some of the relatives. I guess I'll see you guys after the Grand Entry." Jeremiah glanced into a hand mirror. "Man, I wish I had my own eagle feather."

Cody propped himself up on his elbow as Jeremiah strolled out of the tepee. The small round opening at the top of the tepee now revealed gray clouds stacking up in the sky. The air inside was hot, stuffy, and stale.

I could hike down to Elmo and call Mom. Maybe Denver could drive over and pick me up. I ought to be home. They need me to help them put up the hay. I should never have come.

Lord, I know my place. This just isn't my place.

I'm out of step. Everything I do or say is wrong. Lord, this just might be the worst day I've had in my life.

"Cody Wayne!"

He sat up so quickly his head spun. He focused on the daylight beaming through the open doorway where Feather and Honey stood.

"Were you asleep?" Feather asked.

"Oh no, well . . . sort of. I was, you know, thinkin'."

"Doesn't Honey's outfit look awesome?"

The long fringe from Honey Del Mateo's intricately

beaded buckskin dress hung almost to the ground. With black bangs, red ribbon woven into her braids, and dangling bead earrings, she looked like a photograph in *National Geographic*.

"That *is* a great outfit," he mumbled.

"Thanks, Cody."

Still wearing jeans shorts, T-shirt, and knee-high suede moccasins, Feather brushed past Honey and entered the tepee. "Where's Larry and Townie?"

"Larry went to shoot some hoops, and Townie's gone with his grandad."

"Come on, let's go to the barbecue."

"Eh, I'm not hungry. We've been snackin' all afternoon."

"I'll save you a place in the grandstand then," Feather announced. "I want you to explain everything that's going on."

"Yeah, sure . . . whatever," he muttered.

The girls had been gone about ten minutes, and Cody was once again sprawled on his back when a sudden thunderclap made him jump. A couple of drops of water splashed on his face.

Oh, great! Now it's going to rain!

Three

✺

*I*t wasn't until drum beats filled the air that Cody struggled to his feet and stared out the open doorway of the twenty-foot-tall tepee. While occasional lightning flashed from the dark clouds stacked against the Rockies, the rain had done no more than barely settle the fine reddish-brown dust of the Montana hillside.

He stepped outside the tent and took a deep breath. The air tasted clean but still warm. All the tepees, campers, and tents around him looked deserted. He could see the temporary lights from the arena, even though it wouldn't be dark for an hour. He jammed his hands into the back pockets of his Wranglers.

Cody tugged on his black beaver felt cowboy hat, looped his coiled rope over his shoulder, and meandered through the unorganized sprawl of rigs and tents. The makeshift arena covered the hillside next to the basketball courts. Bleachers were no more than lawn chairs and the rear ends of pickups backed up to the bare dirt field that served as a dancing ground.

Because Cody's tepee was on higher ground than the facility, he could look down and see the entire crowd as he approached. The sunlight broke through the clouds and reflected in a wild, exciting abandon from the multicolored beads, feathers, and buckskin of hundreds of costumes. As he approached, he could hear not only the drums but the flutes as well. Each of the dancers sported a white placard on the left arm with black numbers as identification for the judges.

Cody spotted Jeremiah at the center of the grounds near the tall pole that sported an American flag. He thought he could see Eddie huddle with a team of players around a large drum. He couldn't tell if Honey was playing a flute or not. He stayed well away from the crowd, choosing to lean against the hood of a dark blue Ford pickup.

Feather and Larry are somewhere. Of course, so is Daniel Old Horn. He probably still wants revenge. Why does everyone have to get even?

"What do you think you're doin'?"

The angry voice from behind him sent a chill down Cody's back. His coiled rope dropped to his hand as he spun around to face Daniel Old Horn, in beaded buckskin. Standing uphill from Cody, the older boy looked taller.

"Oh . . . hi, Daniel. I was, you know, watching the events in the arena. I, eh, thought you'd be dancing."

"Yeah, I'll bet you did. That's why you came to rip me off."

"What do you mean?"

"As if you didn't know—this is my dad's rig." Daniel pointed to the dark blue Ford.

"It is? Actually, I was just looking for Feather and Larry. I wanted to sit with them."

"You and me have something to finish." Old Horn stepped closer.

"Danny, I apologized already for what happened at the basketball courts."

"You made me look stupid."

"I didn't plan on doing it."

Daniel stepped within a foot of Cody and clenched his right fist. "You ever had your nose broken, Clark?"

Cody took a deep breath and tried to keep his voice low. He took a step back. His voice quivered a little. "Twice. The first time a calf I was ropin' kicked me in the face. The second time was when I got bucked off a horse into some rocks. How about you, Danny? Have you ever been horsewhipped by a stiff nylon rope?" Cody countered.

Old Horn glanced down at the rope in Cody's right hand. "You're lucky I've got my buckskins on. You aren't worth getting them dirty."

Cody felt the sweat roll down his forehead. He never took his eyes off Daniel's. "Well, in that case, I'm going to find Feather and Larry."

"You stay away from my Honey!" Danny shouted.

Halfway down the slope of the campground, Cody turned around and hollered, "What are you so worried about, Danny? You don't think I'm competition to you, do you?"

For the first time since their confrontation on the

basketball court, Daniel Old Horn smiled. "Yeah . . . you're right. No girl is dumb enough to choose you over me!"

Cody scooted on down the hill. *That's great, Lord. I get out of a jam by putting myself down.*

Larry and Feather were fairly easy to spot as Cody approached the dancing ground. In the crowd of four hundred people watching three hundred dancers, he could not see more than two dozen people who were not Native Americans.

Cody slipped up behind the old bright orange Dodge pickup where Feather and Larry were lounging in white molded-plastic lawn chairs propped up in the back. "Hey, guys, how's it going?"

"Well, if it isn't the late Cody Wayne Clark," Feather snapped.

"We thought maybe you went home," Larry teased as Cody climbed up in the back of the pickup and plopped down on the side rail.

"Yeah, right. I took a little nap, that's all. Then I got delayed on the way down."

"You missed a great barbecue."

"Whose truck is this? They don't mind if we sit here, do they?"

Feather stood up and shaded her eyes from a bright setting sun that now peeked through the quickly scattering clouds. "Nah, it belongs to Eddie's folks. They parked it here so we would get a good view."

"How's the program?"

"I don't understand it too well," Larry reported. "Is Townie winning?"

"They aren't competing yet. This is just the Grand Entry."

"It's incredible," Larry continued. "I didn't know people still dressed up like this."

Feather stared down at her knee-high moccasins. "Cody, how do you think I'd look in a buckskin dress?"

"Pale."

Cody jerked to the left to avoid Feather's clenched fist aimed at his stomach and promptly tumbled out of the pickup into the dirt.

"Cody, are you all right? I'm sorry," she called.

When he glanced up from the ground, he saw both Feather and Larry, openmouthed, staring down at him. Cody began to laugh.

"What's so funny?" Feather asked.

Cody's right hand held his stomach while his left pointed at Feather.

"Are you laughing at me, Cody Wayne?" Her green eyes narrowed. "Why's he laughing, Larry?"

Cody tried to stop laughing, but then he burst out in hysterics.

"He must have hit his head on a rock. That happened to my brother one time when he fell out of his seat at a Pacers game. My mom had to take him out to the concessions and buy him a caramel apple before he settled down," Larry reported.

"What's the matter, Cody?" She clenched both of her fists. "You answer me right now!"

Cody sat up and leaned his back against the pickup tire. He clutched his side and bit his lip.

"Did you hurt your side?" Feather called.

Cody shook his head. Then a snicker burst into a full-fledged guffaw as he struggled to his feet.

"Are you all right?" Feather's voice was softer now.

"I'm okay . . . really. It was just funny. I couldn't stop laughing."

Cody climbed back into the pickup bed.

"Are you going to tell us what you were laughing about?" Larry demanded.

"It's nothing."

Feather put her hands on her hips and scowled at him. "What do you mean, nothing? It was obviously something."

"Actually it was everything."

"Which is it, Clark—nothing or everything?"

"Both. See, when I left the tepee, I was wishing I was anywhere on earth but here. I mean, I've been humiliated, embarrassed, and in a fight. But I headed down here because I finally figured I'd gone through the worst, and things would get better. But then Danny Old Horn threatened me, and I only escaped by putting myself down. So I crawled up here to lick my wounds and hide, and what happens?"

"I try to slug you."

"Yeah, and I ducked the punch."

"Yeah, but why were you laughing?" Larry pressed.

"Well, when I sat down up here, I said, 'Lord, at least things can't get any worse.' Then I fell out of the truck!" Cody began to chuckle again.

Larry stared at him for minute. "I don't get it," he finally admitted.

"Don't you see? Just when I think nothing can get worse, I fall out of the truck."

"Do you understand what he's talking about?" Larry quizzed Feather.

"I think so."

"I guarantee that if a meteorite falls to earth tonight, it will hit me right on the head."

"Does he need a doctor?" Larry wasn't smiling.

"No, but he definitely needs to get his mind on something else. Tell us about the dance. Which one is Townie doing now? He's pretty good, isn't he?" she questioned.

"I felt just like Jonah." Cody grinned.

"Who?" she asked.

"You know, Jonah—in the Bible. See, he was in this boat running away from God's purposes when a terrible storm came up at sea. Everyone just knew they were going to drown. Jonah said it was all his fault things were going bad, and if they wanted to save their lives, they should throw him overboard. They reluctantly agreed and tossed him out, and everything grew calm."

"What happened to Jonah?" Feather asked.

"He got swallowed alive by a big fish, but that's not the point. See, just when I figured things—"

"What do you mean, that's not the point? A guy gets swallowed alive, and that's not the point?"

"No . . . it's the point in the Bible, but it's not my point. What I meant was, everything was going so lousy today that my falling out of the truck was like Jonah being thrown overboard. Get it?"

"You're weird, Clark—really weird!" Larry chided.

"Thank you."

"What happened to Jonah?" Feather demanded.

"The giant fish barfed him up on shore, and he went on to—"

"The fish did what?"

"You know . . . barf, vomit, regurgitated him."

"This is really, really gross!"

"He went on to preach to the Ninevites like God wanted him to."

"Can you imagine how horrible he'd smell?"

"Who?" Larry asked.

"This Jonah guy!" she exclaimed.

"He probably took a bath," Cody conceded.

Feather rolled her eyes and wiggled her nose. "I'll bet he did."

"Anyway," Cody continued, "it just struck me funny that everything was going wrong on the same day. What I was thinking was that since this day was shot already, maybe the Lord's allowing everything to go wrong on the same day means that all the rest of the days will be really great."

"What if this is your really great day?" Larry teased.

"Now that's a wonderful thought." Cody stood up in the back of the pickup with the thundering sound of drums booming over the loudspeakers and shouted, "Take your best shot, world! I'm ready. Let's get it over with!"

No one heard a thing he said except Larry and Feather, who both doubled up in laughter.

Cody plopped down in one of the plastic lawn chairs.

"You're in my chair, Cody Wayne," Larry complained.

"So shoot me. What else could go wrong?"

Larry pointed his index finger at Cody and said, "Pow!"

Immediately Cody staggered to his feet and tottered and swayed around the back of the truck. "You got me, Tap Andrews! My whole life is passin' before my eyes."

"Even the first grade?" Feather asked.

"Especially the first grade!" Cody threw his arm around her shoulders. "I'm a goin' fast, Miss Feather. How about one last kiss before I cross over that Great Divide?" *I can't believe I said that! If she tries to kiss me, I'll die!*

"Kiss a bleeding, dying man who's been rolling in the dirt? Get real!" She shoved him off her shoulders. Cody staggered back. His cowboy boots caught in the bed of the pickup, and he tumbled with a whoop to the dirt. This time he landed on his backside.

And this time he, Larry, and Feather all burst out laughing.

When Cody reached over for his black cowboy hat, he noticed three moccasin-encased pairs of feet standing beside the pickup. He rubbed the dust out of his eyes and squinted at Honey Del Mateo, Jeremiah Yellowboy, and Eddie Winterhawk.

"Well, Clark," Jeremiah probed, "it looks like we missed all the action. You showin' 'em how to wrestle a steer—without the steer?"

"Cody's practicing falling out of the back of pickups," Larry announced.

"Actually he's getting quite good at it," Feather added.

Honey's voice dripped with disgust. "That I can see!"

"Did anyone tell him there are no showers out here?" Eddie asked.

Cody struggled to his feet. "Really? You mean I have to stay covered with dirt all weekend?"

"Afraid so, partner." Jeremiah grinned. "Unless you want to swim in a very cold lake."

Cody looked up at Feather and Larry. Then all three burst out laughing.

Eddie shook his head. "Your friends are weird, Yellowboy."

"*My* friends? I thought they were *your* friends!" He grinned.

"No way. Maybe they're Honey's friends."

"I've never seen them before in my life."

The three in buckskins kept staring until Feather, Larry, and Cody were finally able to stop laughing.

"Hey, if you three have calmed down, you want to go shoot some hoops?" Jeremiah suggested. "They have one light over by that hoop near the arena."

Cody pulled off his cowboy hat and ran his fingers through his brown hair. "You saw what happened to me last time."

"Daniel won't be there," Honey reported. "Just us three and you three."

"No body-slamming, Eddie—especially me," Cody exhorted.

"From the looks of you, what would it hurt?" Eddie laughed. "We'll change clothes and meet you down there."

A single halogen portable street light mounted ten feet above the basket provided the only light on the hillside court. The earlier thundershowers had settled the dust, yet left little, if any, mud. The clouds had now disappeared as quickly as they had appeared, taking with them the humidity.

The slightly cool evening air was roofed by a canopy of stars. When the full moon first came up over the granite snowless peaks of the Rockies, it looked ten times its normal size. Moonbeams streaked across Flathead Lake, as if they were aimed straight at the six basketball players.

When Larry Lewis slashed to the basket and bounced off the immovable Eddie Winterhawk, Cody figured the panicked shot didn't have a chance in the world. It glanced high off the backboard and then dropped like a wounded duck through the net, the winning basket.

"Yes!" Larry shouted, giving Feather a high five.

Cody was startled to hear applause. He glanced into the shadows surrounding the court and noticed that several dozen people had gathered to watch the game.

"I didn't know we had an audience," he whispered at Honey.

"Yeah. The game seemed to go quickly."

"A score of 20 to 18 is an exciting game."

"We get a rematch, don't we?" Eddie insisted.

"I'm in," Larry announced.

'Eh . . . sure, I mean, we don't have anything else to do, do we?" Cody asked.

"We could go back to the tepee and play Risk, but Feather would cheat." Jeremiah grinned.

"How about you girls?" Cody asked. "You want to play another?"

Feather raised her eyebrows and glanced at Honey. "Is he saying that somehow girls lack stamina?"

Honey tossed her waist-length, flowing black hair over her shoulders and winked at Feather. "The day I couldn't outrun a bowlegged cowboy would be a sad day." She giggled.

Jeremiah grabbed the basketball and dribbled it on the dirt. "I think you've been dissed, Cody Wayne! I'll shoot for outs."

He threw up a shot from deep beyond the three-point line that had been heel-drawn in the dirt.

Nothing but net.

Even though the night air continued to cool, Cody was soon sweating completely through his black sleeveless T-shirt. By good ball movement, quick sets, and face-up shooting, Larry, Feather, and Cody matched Townie, Honey, and Eddie basket for basket until it was tied at 18 each.

Larry huddled his team at half-court before they brought the ball in.

"Come on, L.B.L.," Jeremiah teased, "bring the ball. There isn't any play on earth that can overcome the aggressive defense of Townie's Tornados!"

"Townie's Tornados? That's the name of your team?" Cody laughed.

"I was thinking about calling us Honey's Hurricanes," Honey Del Mateo announced.

"You've got to be kidding," Eddie boomed. "This team

is Eddie's Eagles! How about you guys? Are you the Pillows?"

"Pillows?"

"You know—Feather's Pillows?"

"Very funny." Feather scowled. "How about Feather's Falcons?"

Cody nodded agreement. "Or how about Cody's Cowboys?"

"Boring, totally boring," Larry insisted. "This team is Larry's Hoosiers!"

"What kind of name is that?" Eddie hooted.

"Are you insulting the best basketball program in the United States?"

"I don't think so." Eddie grinned. "I don't even know what a Hoosier is."

"Neither does anyone else," Feather added. "I say it's Eddie's Eagles against Feather's Falcons."

Heads nodded as Larry pulled Feather and Cody close. "Listen, guys, I'll drive in on Eddie like last game—only this time I'll drop it off to one of you. You take the shot, and we'll all crash the boards for the rebound."

Feather bounced the ball into Larry and then ran for the baseline at the corner of the court. Cody started out under the basket with Eddie but broke to the corner as soon as Larry slashed to the hoop. Eddie stayed back to guard Larry, which left Cody completely alone.

All right, Larry, pass me the ball! Come on!

Instead of bounce-passing it to Cody, Larry leaped toward the basket and tried to finger-roll a shot over Eddie Winterhawk.

The sound of Eddie's wide, strong palm blocking the shot sounded like a bat striking a softball. The basketball flew across the court, took one bounce, and was caught by Honey Del Mateo, well beyond the three-point line. She spun and chucked the ball over Feather's outstretched long, thin arms.

But the ball sailed beyond Eddie's outstretched hands, crashed into the backboard, and dropped through the net.

The small, enthusiastic crowd applauded from the moonlit shadows.

"Bank! I did say bank," Honey laughed.

"All right! We won!" Jeremiah triumphed.

"One to one. We have to play another," Larry challenged as he retrieved the basketball.

"What time is it?" Cody asked no one in particular.

"What difference does it make?" Honey replied. "Have you got a date?"

"Cody have a date!" Feather howled. "He's too embarrassed even to think about being alone with a girl!"

"Hey, are we going to play basketball or stand around discussing Cody's nonexistent love life?" Larry demanded.

"I agree with Larry!" Cody blurted out.

"About basketball or about your love life?" Eddie teased.

"Whoa!" Jeremiah laughed. "Cody's red enough now to become an honorary member of the tribe."

Larry threw his arm around Cody's shoulder. "Don't worry, partner. They're just trying to mess with your mind because they know they're going up against a superior team."

"Superior?" Eddie jibed. "I suppose anyone named Larry Bird Lewis would have trouble living in the real world. Say, wasn't there a guy in the NBA named Bird? Did he ever do much?"

"That did it!" Larry hooted. "That was a crucial error. When they dis Larry Bird, they elevate my game to a higher level. You just thought I was MVP caliber before. Now you will see basketball as it has never been played before!"

Actually the third game turned out to be quite similar to the other two. The score was 18 to 16 when Jeremiah made a three-pointer at the baseline while falling away from Larry's aggressive defense. Someone in the shadows cheered and applauded.

Jeremiah strutted across the court. "And the crowd goes wild!"

"All right," Eddie hollered from under the basket. "One more point, and we're the world champs!"

"World champs?" Feather questioned. "Don't you think you're getting a little carried away?"

"Are you kidding? Someday there'll be a giant statue of me right out by the highway marking the spot where I won the championship. Tourists will flock to see it," Eddie laughed.

"What are they going to build it out of?" Feather glanced around at the dark hillside. "Cow chips?"

Cody studied Eddie's stunned face and was relieved when it broke into a wide smile. "Boy, that would attract the tourists!" he howled.

"Until it rained!" Jeremiah added.

"Hey, it's not over yet!" Larry insisted. "It's our ball. All right, Falcons, let's do the Hoosiers' #26."

Cody glanced at Feather. She shrugged.

"Nobody's playin' nothin'!" a voice boomed from a mass of people huddled in the shadows.

Danny? Lord, I was having so much fun I actually forgot about him. Why does he have to show up now?

Daniel Old Horn came out under the halogen light. "I told you to stay away from Honey!" he growled at Cody.

"I haven't even been guarding her!"

"That's not what I hear!"

"Chill off, Daniel," Honey cautioned. "We have a game to finish."

"You don't." He grabbed Honey's wrist and tugged her toward the shadows.

"Turn loose of me!"

"Turn loose of her!" Cody blurted out. His voice sounded short of breath.

"Says who?" Danny thundered. "I'll settle up with you later!"

Eddie's thick, callused right hand slapped down on Danny's shoulder. "Come on, Danny, let go!"

"Whose side are you on?" Daniel demanded.

A wide, happy smile flashed across the big boy's face. "I'm on Honey's side!"

"Yeah, well, it's a long weekend." He released Honey and stepped away from Eddie's grip. Then he waved a clenched fist at Cody. "I'll get even with you. You can count on that!"

"Why?" Feather prodded.

Daniel glared at them as he stormed toward the campers and tepees.

"Sorry," Honey apologized. "Danny's a good guy really. Just very insecure. He's had a rough life."

"He seems cocky to me," Larry observed.

"That's a show. Everything becomes a threat when you don't have any self-confidence. Anyway, thanks for the rescue."

"Are we going to finish this game?" Larry dribbled the ball between his legs.

"Yeah . . . and it's 18 to 19, with us leading," Jeremiah informed him.

"But we have the ball!" Feather proclaimed.

Larry coached, "Remember, guys, Hoosier #26."

"Sure, whatever," Cody mumbled.

Feather tossed the ball in to Cody. He quickly passed the ball to Larry, who slashed by Feather's pick to ditch Jeremiah, who was guarding him closely.

"Switch!" Jeremiah called, and immediately Honey pursued Larry. She leaped back and cut off the lane, forcing Larry to the baseline without a shot. As he started to pull up, the basketball squirted off his left foot.

"No!" Larry shouted, diving to save the ball from going out of bounds.

With his head barely off the ground, Larry scooped up the ball before it rolled across the out-of-bounds line. With his back to the basket, he flung the ball high in the air over his head before he tumbled to the dirt.

Cody and Eddie stood under the basket and stared, mouths open. The ball sailed into the backboard, slammed onto the front rim, recoiled three feet into the air, and then dropped into the net.

"Yes!" Larry shouted from the ground. "Yes!"

"I don't believe that," Jeremiah groaned. "We had him covered. There's no way he could make that shot."

"Is that Hoosier #26?" Honey teased.

"Am I good, or what? Oh, man, I wish we had that on video. That would have made 'Sports Center Highlights' for sure!"

"It was total luck!" Jeremiah insisted.

"Good teams always find a way to win!" Larry bragged.

"Have you ever seen anything like that?" Eddie asked.

Cody shook his head. "But it doesn't surprise me. Larry wants to win so bad, he can get the ball to the hoop by sheer force of will."

Honey pulled up her long black hair and stacked it on her head. "Really?"

"That's the way it seems."

"Hey, let's head up to our outfit and have a Gatorade," Jeremiah suggested. "I think we're out of cookies. But we have chips—oh, man, have we got chips!"

Honey wandered toward the shadows at the edge of the court away from the others. "I've got to go see Danny."

Feather held her tie-dyed T-shirt away from her stomach and fanned it back and forth. "Why?"

"Hey, I like him. . . . He's okay. Really."

"You know what?" Feather waited for Honey to look her in the eyes. "When I was eleven, I had a boyfriend named Van Brenner. My mother didn't like him, and I spent six months telling her what a great guy he was."

"So?"

"So at the end of six months, I woke up one morning and realized my mother was right. He was a jerk. I figure if you have to keep explaining to your friends and family that a person is all right, maybe he's not. Take Mr. Nice here—"

"Who?" Honey asked.

Cody stared down at his tennis shoes. *Don't embarrass me again, please.*

"Cody. That's the name my mother gave him. I never had to say anything to her about him."

Honey looked Cody right in the eyes. "Yeah, well . . . Cody's your guy, Feather. Maybe there aren't enough Mr. Nice's to go around."

"That's not true!" Feather blurted out.

"Oh?" Honey leaned her brown face close to Feather's pale, freckled one. "Which part isn't true?"

"About there not being enough nice guys."

"Anyway, I'm going to see Danny. I'll be up to the camper later." She spun on the dirt court and trotted into the evening darkness.

The other five hiked up the side of the mountain, Jeremiah Yellowboy leading the way. They had just marched single file between two travel trailers when a white-haired man suddenly appeared in one of the lighted trailer doorways.

"Which team won," he called out, "the Eagles or the Falcons?"

"The Falcons!" Larry reported, spinning his basketball on his finger.

"I thought perhaps the Eagles would win."

"We played them close," Eddie told him.

"Yes . . . well, what I meant was that since we're only a short distance from Eagle Island, I thought the Eagles would win."

Jeremiah stepped up close to the old man's door. "What do you mean, Eagle Island?"

"That tiny island out in the bay. When I was young, there were several nests of bald eagles out there. They say they're all gone now. Perhaps that's why the Eagles didn't win."

The five hiked on to Jeremiah's grandfather's tepee in silence. As they approached the opening, Eddie stopped to stare out into the darkness toward Flathead Lake.

"Are you thinking what I'm thinking?" Jeremiah asked.

"Yeah." Eddie nodded. "I sure would like to have my own eagle feather before Sunday night."

Four

*C*ody felt dirty when he woke up Saturday morning.

He *was* dirty.

The night air had chilled around midnight, and he had crawled into his sleeping bag fully clothed. But by 5:00 A.M. he woke up sweating, and the grime from his tumble off the pickup and three basketball games made him feel sticky and uncomfortable. He lay on top of the bag for another hour. Then he got up, washed his face, hands, and feet in a basin of very cold water, and joined Jeremiah and his grandfather at a propane grill where breakfast was being cooked.

"Hey, Cody, Grandpa says he once went out to Eagle Island and brought back a whole handful of eagle feathers!"

"When?"

The old man stared out across the campers and tepees. His thick gray hair hung out from under a Seattle Mariners baseball cap and reached his shoulders. His dark brown leathery face had deep creases, much like wagon ruts in the soil after a wave of pioneer wagons have crossed.

"It was October 21, 1937. It was cloudy, and there was a cold wind from the northwest. It snowed the next day."

"Wow, you remember all of that?" Cody quizzed.

"I remember even the bitter taste." Mr. Yellowboy nodded.

Jeremiah held his hands above the propane stove and rubbed them together. "Taste? What did you taste, Grandpa?"

"The feathers."

"You ate eagle feathers?" Jeremiah gulped. "I thought you had to pluck a bird before you ate it."

The old man winked at Cody. "My grandson believes anything. He would make a fine employee of the BIA, don't you think?"

Cody ran his hands up and down his bare arms. "You didn't eat the feathers?"

"Nor did I eat eagle. I carried the feathers in my teeth all the way back to the shore."

"Why?"

"Because I needed my hands to swim."

"Swim? You swam over to Eagle Island?" Jeremiah poured boiling water into a white Styrofoam cup and began stirring in chocolate mix.

"It was the only way I could get there."

"You mean they didn't have a marina or boats or anything in 1939?"

"1937," he corrected. "Oh, they had boats. But they told me they didn't rent boats to my kind."

"Your kind?" Jeremiah stepped back. "What kind were you back then?"

Mr. Yellowboy shook his head and gazed across the lake at the distant mountains. "You know . . . many want to go back to the old days. There are some old days that I do not want to go back to."

"They wouldn't rent you a boat because you were an Indian, right?" Cody asked.

"I still am Indian."

"But they let you rent a boat now, don't they?" Cody asked.

"Oh yes. In fact, the manager of the marina was here last night looking for business. They are quite happy to take our money now."

"Are you going to rent a boat and go out there?" Jeremiah asked.

"No. I will never rent a boat at that marina."

Cody stirred himself a cup of hot chocolate, too. "It's not the same people who run it as in 1937, is it?"

"Oh no." The old man smiled but was silent for several moments. "These folks seem quite nice and friendly. But it is my tiny protest before the winds, the mountains, and the lake that I have not forgotten how I was treated. The blessings of the present are much sweeter when the bitter taste of the past is still in one's memory."

Larry plodded out of the tepee dragging a green wool army blanket over his shoulders and holding a basketball under his arm. He scooted up next to Jeremiah.

"So the feathers tasted bitter?" Cody asked.

"Yes. And the waters were quite cold. I was blue when

I got to shore. I considered dying when I was in the water but thought better of it."

"What did you do with those feathers, Grandpa?" Jeremiah queried. "Are those the ones Eddie and I get to borrow?"

"Oh no. I took those to your grandmother's father when I asked him if I could marry his daughter."

"You traded him feathers for Grandma?"

The old man laughed. It was a deep laugh, a laugh that vaulted decades, perhaps centuries. "No, no! I gave him eagle feathers, a spotted pony, six blankets, twenty pounds of pistachio nuts, a radio, and a subscription to *Reader's Digest* magazine. And," he tossed his arm around Jeremiah's shoulder, "I did not buy your grandmother. Those were thank-you gifts to her father for his permission to marry her."

"Do you think there may be some eagle feathers still out there?" Cody asked.

"The eagles have been gone for years. I don't think there are any more feathers."

"Hey, are you talking about me?"

Feather strolled up from the camper, her long hair in braids that were woven with turquoise and silver ribbons.

"If you had a tan, you could pass for Kiowa," Mr. Yellowboy announced.

"Really?"

The old man's eyes twinkled somewhere between tease and truth.

"We were talking about eagle feathers," Cody informed her.

"Are we going out to Eagle Island?" she asked.

Jeremiah looked up from his cup with a stylish chocolate mustache on his lip. "Grandpa doesn't think there are any feathers left."

"Well, maybe there's buried treasure out there, and we could find it and become wealthy!" Feather suggested.

Mr. Yellowboy laughed. This time it was more shallow. "You are a very optimistic young lady."

She grinned and wrinkled her nose to a wave of freckles. "It's my gift!"

"What do you think, Grandpa?" Jeremiah probed. "Can we rent a boat and go out to Eagle Island?"

"I will not go with you. It is too far to swim for an old man. I do not think they will rent a boat to you."

"But I thought you said they—"

"It has nothing to do with the color of your skin. I don't think they rent boats to anyone under eighteen. How many want to go?"

"The four of us—and Eddie," Jeremiah replied.

"You will need a large boat, but it won't hurt to ask." The old man grinned. "Get your plates. Breakfast is ready."

"I want to go, too!"

Honey Del Mateo marched into the group. She was barefoot and wore shorts and a fringed suede tank top. She had combed out her hair, and it flowed down her shoulders and back like a thick, black velvet veil.

Jeremiah scooped up a paper plate and moved to be first in line. "Good! That means there will be six of us."

Feather scooted over next to Honey. "Where did you get that bruise on your arm?"

"Oh? I, eh . . ." She crossed her arms and covered the bruise with her hand. "I think I bumped into something in the camper when I came in last night. It was a little late. It's no big deal. What time are we going to Eagle Island?"

"We've got a basketball game," Larry reminded them.

"That's at 9:00. We could go after that," Jeremiah suggested.

"But then we have another game at 2:00," Larry insisted.

Honey filed in line behind Jeremiah. "Only if you win."

Larry bounced his basketball, stirring up a small cloud of dust. "If? If? Of course we'll win."

Jeremiah speared four huge pancakes, looked around at the others, and then put one back on the stack. "It won't take us long to go out there and look around. We'll be back before lunch."

"We could go over our game plan on the way," Larry suggested.

"You guys have game plans for your basketball games?" Honey asked in amazement.

"We have game plans for our game plans!" Feather giggled.

When Larry huddled the Lewis and Clark Squad near the sideline of the dirt court, there was a sly smile on his face. "I scouted them out. The combined vertical leap of the team is one inch! They all dribble looking down and only right-handed. All three of them have trouble making lay-ins unguarded. I think if we keep a fast pace, we can get this over in a hurry. Besides, how tough can a team be that is called the Sleepers?"

Cody glanced over at three heavy-set, brown-skinned boys who wore matching Denver Nuggets T-shirts. "Do you know these guys, Townie?"

"Nope. I think they're from down near Cortez, Colorado. They call themselves the Sleeping Utes."

"Don't let up on them just because we get a big lead," Larry cautioned. "We need to find our rhythm and play to our best level. It will get increasingly difficult as we progress through this tournament."

It was increasingly difficult from the very first play of the game. A boy called Burto took the inbound pass six feet above the three-point line, turned, and threw up a shot over a top-of-the-key-playing Larry Lewis.

Nothing but net.

"A totally lucky shot!" Larry mumbled as he took the inbound pass from Cody. He bounce-passed the ball to Jeremiah and then broke for the basket. The pass back to him was right on target, and he had an easy lay-in.

This was followed by another long three-pointer from the Sleeping Utes. Next possession, the pass was in to Cody, and he made a five-foot jump shot off the backboard.

"All right!" Larry shouted.

Each team made two more shots. Feather called a time-out from the bench.

"I'm getting winded. Go in for me," Cody told her.

"You aren't winded, Mr. Nice, but I will go in for you. We need to do something different or we'll lose."

"Lose? We're matching them point for point," Larry protested. "They can't stop us!"

"They don't need to stop us. We're matching them basket for basket but not point for point. They've got twelve; we've got eight."

"They don't need defense," Townie groaned. "Just keep popping the threes, and they'll get to 20 before us."

"We've got to stop them and hit a couple of threes ourselves," Feather added.

With his hands on his hips, Larry leaned into the huddle. "Let's go to a half-court press. Get in their faces the second they bring the ball in. One on one, no one drops back."

Cody ran his fingers through his thick brown hair. "What if they break around us?"

"Try to drop back, but don't foul them. Let's see if they can make lay-ins. Even if they get a jump, follow them clear to the basket. But don't double-team. If we leave our man, they'll bounce it back and can the three." Larry turned to Jeremiah. "Townie, you take a three-pointer every time you get a clear look at the basket."

On the Sleeping Utes' next possession, Feather, with hands and braids flying, swarmed the ball handler near mid-court. He tossed a hurried pass. Larry intercepted the ball near the top of the key and slashed toward the basket. He was quickly double-teamed, leaving Townie open in the corner.

A bounce pass.

A classic high-arcing shot.

The sweet, sweet sound of net.

The score was tied at 17 when Larry called their second and last time-out. Jeremiah limped over to the huddle.

"Townie, what happened?"

"He came down on my foot on purpose. Did you see that?"

"How does it feel?"

"Like a 200-pound shot put was dropped on my toe."

"But you can still shoot, right?" Larry prodded.

"We've got to get the ball first. I can't guard them close. I've got to sit down. Put in the cowboy."

"But . . . but we need a three-pointer!"

"Let Feather shoot it."

Larry took a deep breath, then blew out the air slowly. "Right. Feather-girl, you take the three. But we can't give them a clear shot."

The ball bounced in to Cody's man.

Okay, buddy, no easy shots out here.

The boy had his back to Cody, faked right, turned to the left. Cody stayed with him until the boy lowered his shoulder and leaned into him.

Cody leaned forward, and the boy quickly threw his shoulder into Cody's chin and charged ahead. Cody staggered back and fell into the dirt.

The boy with the ball drove up to the basket, and Feather left her man to fill the lane.

"No!" Larry shouted from the other side of the court. "Don't leave your man!"

The boy with the ball quickly bounced it out to the

open teammate. Feather spun in her red-dust-coated black canvas tennis shoes, took two steps, and leaped into the air like a high jumper.

The blocked shot reflected off her thin hand and bounced to the top of the key where Cody was still picking himself up off the dirt. He snatched up the ball.

Feather and Townie are covered. I'll dribble back and wait for them.

A voice from the sideline shouted, "Shoot the ball, Cody Wayne!"

As the third Sleeper raced toward him, Cody flung up the basketball in an awkward shot that caused him to stumble sideways.

"No!" Larry yelled as he tried to push for position under the basket. The ball sailed like a line drive toward the basket. It glanced off the front of the orange rim, slammed into the backboard, bounced high off the front rim, hit the backboard extremely low, spun one complete circle around the rim, then laid over and died.

In the net.

"Yes!" Larry yelled.

The victorious Lewis and Clark Squad gathered at the sidelines, and two other teams immediately took the court. Eddie Winterhawk had joined Jeremiah in the huddle.

"That was the ugliest winning shot I have ever seen in my entire life!" Larry bellowed.

"Thank you!" Cody grinned. "That was a great block, Feather. I didn't know you could jump that high."

"I can fly." She lifted her nose slightly into the air. "I learned that jump in ballet."

Eddie wore a sheepish grin. "You took ballet?"

"Yeah, and she also took karate," Cody added.

"So did I," Eddie added.

"You took karate?"

"No, ballet."

"You t-took . . . what?" Cody stammered.

Eddie turned to Jeremiah and shook his head. "He believes anything. How did we ever lose a war to these guys?"

"I think all our victories wore us out," Jeremiah laughed. "It's tiring to win all the time."

"All right, no more cowboy and Indian jokes," Cody protested.

Larry stirred up dust by dribbling the ball on the sidelines. "Anyway, we won—even though Cody took that shot when I told him not to."

"All I could hear was Townie yelling for me to shoot."

"Don't blame me. I didn't yell. It was Eddie."

"Eddie? I shot because Eddie yelled at me?"

"Hey, you won the game, didn't you? Is that all the thanks I get? Maybe I should let you row the boat."

"What do you mean, row the boat?" Jeremiah asked.

"Honey and I went down to rent a boat, like you asked us to, but they wouldn't let us rent anything but an old rowboat."

"A rowboat?"

"We're too young for motorboats. We could rent a paddle boat, but we'd need three of them at twelve dollars each. The rowboat was only ten dollars. That's about a buck sixty-five each."

"Six of us can fit in one boat?" Larry quizzed.

"We'll find out, won't we?" Eddied answered. "Honey went back to the camper to fix us some lunch."

Larry spun the basketball on the middle finger of his right hand. "Lunch? We'll be back to rest up for the two o'clock game, won't we?"

Eddie rubbed his broad brown nose with the palm of his left hand. "Eh . . . probably. Honey just thought it would be fun to have a picnic out there. I'll go back and wait by the boat."

Cody wore boots, jeans, a black PRCA National Finals sleeveless T-shirt, and his cowboy hat. The others wore shorts, T-shirts, and tennies.

Cody carried his rope in his right hand.

Honey carried a small black case.

Feather carried a large brown paper sack.

Jeremiah carried a small duffel bag.

Larry carried his basketball.

They had just hiked past the portable outhouses and were waiting for traffic to pass them on the highway when someone shouted, "Where do you think you're going?"

"We're going to—" Cody began.

"Not you, Festus. I'm talking to Honey!" Daniel barked.

Festus? Why did he call me Festus?

"We're just going on a picnic cruise."

"Without me?"

"You're welcome to join us," Honey invited.

Cody shifted his weight from one boot to the other. *No . . . we are not taking Danny!*

"No way! A picnic with these losers would be about as much fun as cleaning a Porta-potty."

Cody tried to hold back a glare. *Yes! Thank You, Lord.*

Daniel reached out and grabbed Honey by the arm. "You aren't goin' either!"

"Don't, Danny!" Honey winced. "That hurts!"

Cody gripped his coiled rope. *That's how she got that bruise!*

"You don't have big Eddie to bail you out this time."

"How about a little Feather?" Feather huffed. Before Daniel could respond, Feather spun and kicked him squarely in the stomach with the heel of her tennis shoe.

Daniel released Honey, took one step back, and sat right down in the dirt, trying to catch his breath.

"Next time I kick lower," Feather snarled.

"Was that karate or ballet?" Larry asked.

"I can't . . . breathe!" Daniel choked.

"Just relax," Feather instructed. "You'll get your breath back in a minute."

"He might not have a minute." Jeremiah pointed to the ground. "He just sat down on an ant den."

"There's a break in the traffic. Let's make a run for it," Larry called out.

Honey started across the road and then glanced back. "Danny, I, eh . . . are you okay?"

Daniel Old Horn staggered to his feet and slapped ants off his jeans.

Honey yelled, "I'll see you when we come back!"

"Hey! It's them!" Larry shouted as he sprinted after a red pickup that sped down the highway.

"Larry!" Cody yelled. "Get out of the road!"

Larry ran for fifty yards with the basketball tucked under his left arm, then veered off to the side of the road, grabbed up a handful of gravel, and flung it at the departing pickup a quarter of a mile down the highway.

Cody and the others jogged up to a panting Larry Lewis.

"That's the guy who stole my basketball!"

"I thought you said they were pulling a boat," Jeremiah reminded him.

"That was the pickup! They must have parked the trailer."

Cody tugged Larry down off the shoulder of the highway. "Maybe it's another red Dakota. It's a popular color."

"I tell you it's them! They had Utah plates."

"Well, even if it was, you can't catch them on foot," Cody put in.

"What would you do if you caught up with them?" Feather asked.

"I'd make them give me back my basketball."

Jeremiah turned around and walked backwards. "How would you make them?"

"Eh . . . well, I'd say, if you don't give back my basketball, Cody will punch you in the nose, Eddie will break your neck, and Feather will kick you in the stomach, and I'll, eh, . . . shove bamboo under your fingernails!"

"Whoa, the vigilantes!" Jeremiah hurrahed. "That kid in the red Dakota just prolonged his life."

"Only for a while," Larry insisted. "I will get him!"

Feather raised her light brown eyebrows. "Oh?"

"They parked the trailer and jet skis around this lake somewhere. All I have to do is find them."

"It's a big lake," Jeremiah observed. "I think it's about thirty miles long and eight miles wide, but the shoreline would be several times that long."

"How many days would it take to hike around it?" Larry inquired.

"About two weeks!" Cody suggested.

"Why don't we take our boat around the shore, and I can look for my basketball?"

"Row a boat? No way!" Jeremiah protested. "That would take a month."

"Well, I'm going to find my basketball! No one steals a basketball from Larry Lewis and gets away with it!"

Eddie stood at the end of the dock near a large, wide, dark green wooden rowboat that curved up out of the water both in the bow and in the stern.

"What kind of rowboat is that?" Larry gasped.

"Oh, they usually have them for running the river. The marina must have gotten a good deal on them or something," Honey reported.

Eddie held the boat steady as the others boarded.

"How many will it hold?" Feather quizzed.

"The man said they can put ten adults in one," Eddie responded.

Larry climbed over the edge and scooted toward the back. "It sure is big!"

Feather pointed toward the middle of the boat. "Do they always have one of these?"

Cody scooted up closer to the boat and peeked in to see a four-foot-diameter drum lying flat in the middle.

"That's mine," Eddie informed her.

"You're bringing your drum?" Feather asked.

"I thought since we're going to be on Eagle Island, I should play the 'Eagle Song,'" Eddie explained.

"Why?" Feather quizzed.

"To attract eagles," Honey replied. "And I brought my flute in this case."

"And I brought my dancing jacket," Jeremiah added.

Cody grabbed an oar and sat on one side of the drum. Eddie plopped down on the other. Honey and Feather settled in at the front of the boat, Jeremiah and Larry at the rear.

"All right, matey," Larry hollered, "cast off! Batten down the hatches, hoist the sail, walk the poop deck—"

"Toss him overboard, Townie, if he keeps that up," Cody said.

"What's a poop deck anyway?" Larry mused.

"That's where all the seagulls roost!" Jeremiah declared.

"That's gross, Townie!" Feather cried.

"Thank you."

Although Eagle Island was only half a mile from shore and the water was fairly calm, Cody thought it took an extremely long time to row out to it.

The island was covered with short pines, stunted firs, and granite boulders. They circled around to the left and found a muddy beach on the other side of the island. Near a large half-submerged boulder, they ran the rowboat aground.

Larry tried unsuccessfully to dribble his ball in the packed mud. "Hey, this whole island isn't any bigger than our lot back in Halt."

"Did they tell you how Halt got its name?" Honey quizzed.

"Oh, man, here we go again. What is this?" Larry groaned. "Everybody on earth has a story about Halt's name."

"Yes, but mine is the real one, of course." Honey tried to stop a giggle.

"Yeah, right. Well, what's the story according to Honey Del Mateo?"

"It comes from a Nez Perce word, *Ha-elt-wai.*"

"*Ha-elt-wai?*"

"Yes, it means ladybug," she announced.

"Ladybug! I live in Ladybug, Idaho?" Larry moaned.

"Well, you do know *Lap-wai* means butterfly, don't you?"

"They named all their towns after bugs?"

"What's wrong with that?" Honey demanded.

"How long does this go on?" Larry huffed.

"As long as you keep believing us," Jeremiah laughed.

"Well," Cody said, pointing to a trail through the trees, "are we going to explore the island?"

"That will take about ten minutes," Larry remarked as he pushed ahead of the others and plunged down the trail.

His prediction turned out to be an overestimate. Within a few minutes they had crisscrossed the tiny island, and all sat on logs that had been rolled up to a rock fire circle in the small clearing.

"Did you see any eagles?" Feather asked the others.

"I didn't see anything alive," Honey reported.

Jeremiah's voice sounded very deep—and phony. "Yes, but did you see anything dead?"

"Don't you guys start that with me again!" Feather protested. "You should have heard them down in that coulee behind Eureka Blaine's horse ranch. They can be so childish!"

Jeremiah picked up a small stone and bounced it into the empty ring of rocks. "Hey, all I meant was that a dead eagle's feather is as good as a live one's."

"What do we do now?" Cody asked.

"I think we ought to go over our basketball game plan. Eddie and Honey can play defense, and we could—"

Honey tossed her long black braids over her shoulders. "What is he—Mr. Basketball?"

"Oh, you've heard of me?"

"We're going to play the 'Eagle Song,'" Eddie announced.

"What are *we* supposed to do?" Larry asked.

"You, Cody, and Feather will need to climb the tallest pines with gunny sacks and wait for the eagles to come in and land. Then stuff them in the sacks and climb down. We'll pluck a few feathers and turn them loose."

"Yeah, right. I've been on snipe hunts before."

"More than once?" Eddie prodded.

"I only held the sack once." Larry lay back on a log and started tossing the basketball straight up in the air and catching it. "Really, what should we do?"

"Just sit back and relax," Honey suggested.

"Larry doesn't relax well," Cody teased.

"Why don't you go hunt for buried treasure?" Feather suggested.

"You're right. Some old prospector might have been trying to escape highwaymen and stashed his loot under a big rock on Eagle Island. Then a storm came up, and he drowned trying to swim back to the mainland in the dark. The canvas bags would have rotted by now, but the nuggets will be there. What's the price of gold this week? Is it still at $385 an ounce?"

Eddie's broad forehead wrinkled. "Is he serious?"

"Oh, yeah. He even knows what he'll do with it when he finds it," Cody reported.

"I'll invest it in mutual funds. A varied portfolio, of course."

"Go for it!" Feather called out.

"I think I will." Larry stood up and dribbled his ball toward the north shore of the tiny island.

Eddie set his big drum up over the top of the fire circle at the center of the island. Jeremiah pulled off his T-shirt and slipped on the beaded buckskin jacket. Honey pulled out her flute. It looked like a foot-long stick with holes in it.

Soon the drum began to pound, the flute tones drifted

through the trees, and Jeremiah Yellowboy danced in tennis shoes.

Feather came over and sat on the log next to Cody. "Is it all right if we talk while they're doing that?"

"I think so," Cody replied.

"It's kind of neat, isn't it?"

"Yeah. I wonder if this was the way it was done a hundred years ago?"

"One time when we lived in a commune in Oregon," she reflected, "there was a family from India. The man played a flute every evening when the sun set. Then there was a guy from Scotland who woke us up at 5:00 A.M. playing a Beach Boys song on his bagpipe."

"Are you kidding me?"

"No. It was something to wake up to—a bagpipe version of 'Barbara Ann.'"

"I guess so."

"Anyway, it's kind of neat to hear other people's cultural traditions and stuff. Is the name Clark English?"

"Yeah. My ancestors came over before the Revolution. At least that's what I was told. How about yours, Feather?"

"My folks don't believe in stuff like that."

"Don't believe in what?"

"You know, looking up family trees and all that. They said we are all on our own and have the ability to succeed or fail regardless of our ancestry. I don't know where my grandparents came from. I don't even know my grandparents."

"Your mom and dad still won't talk to your grandparents?"

"My mom and dad still won't speak to each other."

"Has your mom heard from your dad at all?"

"Nope. I guess he's happy up in Dixie with that other woman."

Cody didn't respond, but listened to the drum and flute.

He heard Feather clear her throat. "Cody, do you think your God could straighten out my dad?"

Cody sat up. "Oh . . . sure. I mean, God can do anything."

"That's what I thought. I think I'll pray for my dad. Did I tell you my mom said it's all right if I pray? That's cool, isn't it?"

"Yeah. Everyone ought to have the right to pray—if they want to."

"I don't know much about praying, but God will listen to me, won't He?"

Cody nodded his head. *This is your chance, Clark. Ask Feather if she believes in Jesus Christ as Lord and Savior yet. Ask her if she's been thinking about last week's Sunday school lesson. Ask her if she's taking God seriously now. Ask her . . . oh, man . . . Lord, this is hard!*

Cody felt his heart pump with every beat of the drum.

He could feel sweat trickle down his neck.

His tongue seemed to stick in his mouth.

He glanced over and watched as Feather drew a picture in the dirt with a stick.

"Is that a . . . a butterfly?" he asked.

"No. It's an eagle," she announced.

I'll ask her sometime when we're alone. This is not a good time to talk about serious stuff.

He looked around the wooded island. "Hey, here comes Larry!"

Larry jogged along toward the center of the island, dribbling his basketball on the pine needles and carrying something shiny in his left hand. "Hey, look what I found!"

"What is it?" Feather asked.

"A bottle. A very old bottle. Look at this! It's cool, huh?"

Cody took the small, clear glass bottle from Larry. "It's handblown. See how uneven the thickness is?"

"It's marked on the side," Larry observed. "What do you suppose that is?"

"O.O.C. & Co." Cody shrugged. "Mrs. Henry down at the hardware collects old bottles. You ought to talk to her and find out what she knows."

"I already figured it out." Larry smiled. "The guy who buried the gold nuggets was sick when he got here, and he took this medicine and started feeling better, so he tried to swim back. But he cramped up halfway back and drowned."

"Quite a story!" Feather laughed.

"It's my gift." Larry plopped down on the log next to Cody. "It's kind of cool having the drum and flute playing in the background all the time."

"Yeah. That music seems to fit this island," Cody agreed.

"I'm thinking maybe they should stop playing for a while."

"Why's that?" Feather asked.

"'Cause when the buzzards start circling, it's time to change the tune, right?" Larry suggested.

"Buzzards?" Cody looked up at the small patch of blue sky above the clearing to where Larry was pointing. The silhouettes were unmistakable. "Buzzards! Those aren't buzzards! Those are eagles! Five bald eagles!"

Five

◉

*T*ownie!" Cody shouted. "Look up there! There's five of them!"

Jeremiah Yellowboy ceased his dance and gawked at the small circle of blue sky. "Wow! It actually works! Is this cool or what?"

Larry's basketball rolled across the forest floor as he observed the big birds circle. "This is kind of weird," he mumbled.

Eddie halted his beating of the drum and stood up to gape. "I've played this song a lot of times and never had an eagle show up—let alone five."

Honey shaded her eyes with her hand. "I've never seen five eagles together in my life."

"Yeah, I thought they were loners," Cody added. "You see a pair every once in a while, but never five of them."

Jeremiah flailed his arms. "Hey . . . they're breaking up!"

"Keep playing," Feather shouted. "You have to keep playing!"

Eddie dropped back down to his knees to beat the drum. Honey, still staring upward, lifted the stick flute to her lips and resumed the haunting melody. Jeremiah's dance was much slower, since his head was thrown back toward the top of the pines.

Larry laid back on a log and propped up his head with the basketball. "Cody, is this some sort of magic? You can't just play a song and have eagles appear."

"Maybe this is an enchanted island," Feather suggested. "Did you ever read C. S. Lewis's Narnia Tales?"

Cody looked into Feather's intense green eyes. "Yeah! They're great. I didn't know you read them."

"My mother said there was a lot of Christian symbolism in them that I should ignore, whatever that means. Anyway, they were fun. So maybe this is an enchanted island where the animals talk."

"There aren't any animals here," Larry reported from his reclining position.

"There are eagles," she maintained.

"I still think it's kind of weird," Larry insisted. "Is this a psychic thing? What do you think, Cody?"

"I figure that over the centuries the Nez Perce people learned a combination of sounds from the flute and drum that attracts eagles. Those birds probably hear a whole lot more than we do."

"Vibrations!" Feather blurted out. "I think birds can pick up vibrations."

"Are you guys saying a certain tune could attract a certain type of bird?" Larry plucked the ball out from under his head and tried to palm it with his left hand.

"My grandpa has a sound machine in his garden that repels birds," Cody reported. "Why not a sound that attracts them?"

"And I say it's really strange." Larry attempted to balance the basketball on his nose. "They just keep circling and circling but don't come down any lower. They don't land; they don't leave. What are they doing?"

"Maybe they're looking for lunch," Jeremiah called out.

"That's a cheery thought." Larry tossed the basketball above his head, caught it, and tossed it up again.

Feather smashed a mosquito on her knee and then stared back up at the eagles. "I wonder if they can talk."

"The eagles?"

"Yeah. In Narnia all the animals can talk. If this was an enchanted island, they might be able to talk."

Jeremiah stopped dancing and waved his hands toward the sky. "Hey, Mr. Eagle!" he shouted. "This is me, Jeremiah Yellowboy. I need you to donate a couple of your feathers."

Honey quit playing the flute and stared up with the others. Eddie kept the big drum beating.

"I don't think they heard—"

A loud squawk from one of the eagles silenced Larry.

Jeremiah remarked, "Now if we only had someone who could translate eagle talk."

"Look, one of them landed in the treetop!" Honey called out.

"Oh, man, I knew we should have you guys in the treetops with gunny sacks!" Jeremiah moaned.

"What do we do now?" Eddie called out above the drum.

"I don't know." Jeremiah shrugged. "I never figured on any eagles actually showing up."

"Maybe we should keep playing and see if they come lower," Honey suggested.

"What would we do if they did?" Feather asked.

"Yeah." Larry stood up and started dribbling the basketball on the mud in time with the tune Eddie was pounding out. "Would we grab them, or would they grab us?"

"I bet Grandpa would know what to do," Townie observed.

Cody jammed his thumbs into the front pockets of his jeans. "Maybe we should try to talk him into coming out."

Even though Jeremiah had stopped dancing, he continued to shift his weight in time with Eddie's drum. "He won't come."

Honey stopped playing the flute and wiped her mouth with the back of her right hand. "Why don't we all go back and ask him what to do?"

Cody stared out toward where the rowboat was run aground. "You mean, row all the way back to the marina and out here again?"

Larry bent low and dribbled the basketball between his legs. "We've got a basketball game at 2:00."

"If we leave, the eagles will leave," Jeremiah warned. "Maybe you three should go back and tell my grandad and then come back out—"

"I don't think so," Cody declared. "This is something *you* have to talk to your grandfather about."

"Well, I, for one, am getting winded," Honey admitted.

Jeremiah let out a deep sigh and then wiped his sweaty forehead. "I'm hungry."

"I'm tired," Eddie grumbled above the boom, boom, boom of the elkhide-covered drum.

Feather tugged at her tiny silver earring and then pointed to the sky. "So are the eagles. They all landed in the treetops."

Jeremiah scooted over to his cousin and knelt by the drum. "What do you say we stop?"

Eddie nodded approval. "As soon as I get to the end of this verse."

"Verse? This song has verses?" Larry mumbled. "It all sounds the same to me."

Eddie played the final beats, lifted his hands, and let them fall to his sides. After a moment of silence, there was a single squawk from the big birds up high in the trees.

"No feathers, no songs—you understand?" Jeremiah called.

"You think they know what you're yelling about?" Feather asked.

"Nope. But I am hungry." Jeremiah slipped off his beaded jacket and pulled on his black and red Chicago Bulls T-shirt.

Feather dug into the big brown paper sack and pulled out a bag of sandwiches. "Maybe they're hungry, too."

Jeremiah grabbed the top sandwich and plopped down on a log. "Well, they don't get my lunch."

Larry opened up his sandwich and stared at its contents. "What do eagles eat anyway?"

Cody waited for the others to choose a bag of chips. "Mice, rabbits, fish, other birds."

"Do they eat baloney?" Larry asked.

"Maybe if there's a dill pickle, Dijon mustard—" Honey giggled.

"And a thin slice of tomato on rye," Eddie added.

"Gourmet eagles!" Feather laughed.

"I suppose they top it off with Perrier?" Larry joined in.

"Oh, any premium bottled water will do," Jeremiah chuckled.

"Hey, speaking of bottled—did you guys see what I found?" Larry pointed to the bottle on a lightning-scarred stump. "I think it's a clue to a buried treasure mystery. It was in the needles under a short stumpy almond tree."

"Almond?" Cody wiped some mayonnaise off the corner of his mouth with the back of his hand. "There aren't any almond trees around here."

Larry waved his sandwich toward the north side of the tiny island. "There's one over there."

"I don't think so," Cody challenged. "No one grows almonds in this country."

"Look, I don't know very much about western trees, but I can spot an almond tree. We had a big one in our backyard in Indiana." Larry put his right foot on top of the basketball and rolled it around on the dirt next to him.

"Show it to me," Cody demanded.

Larry swallowed a large bite of sandwich. "Now?"

"After lunch." Cody shrugged.

Eddie finished off the last sandwich.

Feather pulled the baloney out of hers and ate it meatless.

Honey devoured three bags of chips.

Cody gulped his Gatorade in four swallows.

Jeremiah popped four vanilla wafers into his mouth at a time.

Within minutes every scrap of food was gone.

Honey Del Mateo picked up Larry's old bottle and stepped out into the sunlight to examine it. "I think this used to have a cork stopper."

"Probably," Cody agreed.

"I'll bet that bottle has really seen some history," Larry boasted. "If only bottles could talk!"

"Yeah. It would probably say, 'Pick me up, Larry! Pick me up!'" Honey's voice was high and squeaky.

Feather joined in the laughter and took the bottle from Honey. "Hey, I need a bath! I haven't been washed since 1921!'"

Eddie tugged the bottle from her hand. His high-pitched voice was still several octaves below the girls' voices. "'Man, I could use a drink!'" Then he passed it over to Cody.

Cody's first attempt at a squeaky voice sounded like fingernails on a blackboard. "'Hey, have you guys seen that cute little Coke bottle that came by in 1947?'"

Larry snatched the bottle from Cody's hand. "All right, I get the point. Maybe it's good that bottles can't talk. What's the plan now?"

Jeremiah brushed cookie crumbs off the front of his

T-shirt. "Let's go talk to Grandpa—then maybe come back this afternoon."

Larry scooped up his basketball and took a short jump shot into the trunk of a tall pine. "We need to rest up and review our game plan."

"Who are we playing at 2:00?" Cody asked.

"Some team named the Browning Bombers," Larry reported.

"Oh, man, the Bombers!" Jeremiah groaned. "I was hoping we'd be eliminated before we played them."

"You know them?" Larry asked.

Jeremiah stared down at the black shoestrings on his white Nikes. "They make Devin, Rocky, and J. J. seem like wimps."

Larry retrieved his basketball and strolled over to Jeremiah. "You're kidding, right?"

Townie shook his head. "Nope. My cousin got his nose broken playing them last year."

"Which cousin is that?" Cody asked.

"Loaf."

"You have a cousin named Loaf?"

"Yeah. I have a lot of cousins."

"His name is Loaf Yellowboy?"

"No, Loaf Whitebread . . . and if I hear even a chuckle, we'll leave you tied to a tree on this island!"

Cody glanced over at Jeremiah. "Well, at least it's not a boring name like Cody Wayne Clark."

Eddie picked up his drum and propped it on his shoulder. "Are we ready to load up?"

"Not until we inspect Larry's almond tree," Cody replied.

They hiked through the broken limbs and pine needles until they reached the rocks on the north side. From there they could see the marina and the powwow encampment as it stretched up the mountainside.

"Wow, a person could sit on these rocks with binoculars and see everything that's going on," Jeremiah reported.

Eddie squinted his eyes almost shut. "My dad has some binoculars. When we come back, let's bring them."

"Are we really coming back out?" Larry asked.

"Yep. We saw eagles, but we didn't get any feathers," Jeremiah asserted.

Cody squatted down next to the twelve-foot-tall tree. "Larry's right. It is an almond."

"You doubted me?"

"It's the only one I've ever seen or heard of in the wild."

"If a person wanted to bury treasure, it would be good to do it near a tree that is different from all the others, right?" Feather dug with her hand in the dirt at the base of the tree.

"Why don't we bring a shovel when we come back out?" Larry proposed. "We could dig around while they're collecting feathers."

Cody crawled on his hands and knees back under the lowest drooping limb of the almond until he reached its trunk. "This tree needs to be pruned. There's a lot of sucker growth. Hey, you guys want to see something weird?" he called out.

"What is it?" Honey asked. She stooped and tried to peer under the limb.

"Well, this tree trunk grew up against this rock and wedged a bottle like Larry's between them."

Larry dropped down on his hands and knees. "What do you mean?"

"Look. See the opening of that clear little bottle? It's just like yours, only the back of it's wedged tight between the trunk and the boulder. You can't get it out without breaking the bottle."

Feather crawled back in next to Cody. "I think there is something in the bottle."

"All right!" Larry exploded. "Undoubtedly a treasure map!"

"Whatever it is, it's not coming out. There's no way to free the bottle—let alone pull something out."

"Can't you reach in there with your fingers?" Honey asked.

"Not unless your fingers are six inches long and half the size of a pencil," Feather admitted.

"Needle-nose pliers would work," Cody reported as he crawled back out.

"Oh, man," Larry moaned, "we have to come back now with shovel, pliers, binoculars—"

"And a plan for coaxing eagles to give up their feathers!" Jeremiah added.

With talk of treasure maps dominating the conversation, the trip back to the marina seemed shorter. Honey went off to check on Daniel. Eddie found out that his basketball game had been switched to 1:00 P.M. He jogged to the court, carrying his drum on his back.

Cody, Larry, Jeremiah, and Feather lounged on the sleeping bags inside the Yellowboy tepee.

At least three of them lounged.

The fourth paced around carrying a basketball.

"If the Browning Bombers are a physical team, we're going to have to beat them with speed and good passes. Get rid of the ball quickly. Cody, you'll have to muscle in there and get position on the rebounds."

"They'll double-team you on the rebounds," Jeremiah informed him. "They'll scoot you back out of position. They can catch you with an elbow under the rib cage and lift you off your feet."

"Yeah," Larry inquired, "but can they shoot?"

Jeremiah scrunched up a pillow and propped it under his head. "They finished second last year."

"Who finished first?" Feather quizzed.

"Eddie's team. Didn't we mention that?"

Cody sat up. "You mean, if we keep winning, we'll have to play Eddie?"

"Yeah, and he's the littlest guy on his team," Jeremiah reported.

"What?" Larry choked. "There are guys in our league bigger than Eddie?"

A wide grin broke across Jeremiah's face.

"You're pulling our leg, Townie," Cody declared.

"You almost fell for it," Jeremiah laughed. "There isn't a twelve-year-old in North America bigger than Eddie."

"But his team's good, huh?"

"They lost their best outside shooter, but they will play tough," Jeremiah reported. "Eddie doesn't like to lose."

"Neither do I," Larry insisted.

"As if we didn't know. What happens if we win?" Feather quizzed.

"If we win, we don't have a game until tomorrow morning," Jeremiah answered.

"Sunday morning?" Cody stared straight at Jeremiah. "We have a game on Sunday morning?"

"Only if we keep winning."

"I don't play basketball on Sunday mornings."

"It won't conflict with the church service they're holding down at the arena. We can still go to that," Jeremiah argued.

"You know me better than that, Townie. I don't rodeo on Sunday mornings, and I'm sure not going to play basketball."

"Are you serious?" Larry asked. "This is a joke, right?"

"I'm serious, Larry."

Feather, sitting near the center of the tepee, pulled her skinny knees up and wrapped her arms around them. "You think playing basketball on Sunday morning is a sin?"

"Nope, it's just something I don't do," Cody explained. "I haven't made the Lord many promises yet in my life, but that's one of them. I made up my mind when I was eight and competed in my very first Pee Wee Rodeo that I don't compete on Sunday mornings. Ever."

"Maybe we can get the game rescheduled. Eddie's team traded for this afternoon's game."

"Yeah . . . we can ask," Jeremiah conceded. "But the further toward the finals you get, the less flexibility there is."

"Hey, let's concentrate on one game at a time. We've got to beat the Bombers before we do anything else," Cody reminded them. "Townie, did your grandfather have any suggestions for getting those eagles to leave a feather?"

"He said we should build a trap."

"An eagle trap? Isn't that against the law?" Feather cautioned.

"Not for Native Americans," Jeremiah informed her. "We won't hurt them—just pluck a couple feathers."

Feather began to unbraid her hair. "That sounds like it hurts to me."

"Not if we build the trap right."

"What kind of trap?" Larry quizzed.

"We'll make it out of sticky saplings," Jeremiah reported. "Of course, I don't know where to get sticky saplings."

"It's just like the story in the Bible," Cody declared. "Remember that time in Genesis when Jacob was working for Laban in order to marry the pretty younger sister, Rachel, after he was tricked into taking the older, plainer one, Leah, for a wife?"

"What?" Feather choked.

"You've never heard that story? Well, the point I wanted to make was that Jacob made a fence out of sticks with peeled bark, and it was sticky, and some of it stuck to the sheep, and he got to keep them."

"What is he babbling about?" Larry quizzed.

"Cody's right," Jeremiah declared.

"He is?"

"Yeah, Grandad showed me how to make a trap with a small escape opening," Jeremiah explained. "When the eagle pushes through to get free, he'll lose a feather or two on the sticky saplings, provided we pull the bark back after we build the trap."

Feather ran her fingers through her unbraided hair and let it fall across her shoulders. "What I want to know is what happened to the first wife?"

"You mean Leah?"

"Yeah, what happened when this sleazeball Jacob dumped her for her foxy sister?"

"That's not my point," Cody tried to explain.

"Well, it's *my* point!" she huffed.

"He married them both."

"No kidding? That's in the Bible?" Feather gasped.

"Sure. That's the way they did things back then."

"Can I read about it?"

"Hand me my Bible. I'll show you where it is."

Cody began to flip through his black leather Bible. "What I wanted to know is—even if we have a trap, how are we going to coax the eagle to come into it?"

"Bait."

"That's cool." Larry grinned. "We just walk into the bait shop and ask for Purina Eagle Chow or what?"

"He meant for us to use a rabbit or mouse or something," Cody countered.

Feather looked up from reading Cody's Bible. "We are not sacrificing the life of a rabbit!"

"That's what eagles eat."

"But we don't have to help them!"

"Grandpa said fresh roadkill would probably work," Jeremiah offered.

"Oh, yuck. This whole thing is disgusting," Feather groused.

Cody glanced over at her. "You mean the story of Jacob and Rachel?"

"No! This roadkill trap! You guys aren't really going to do that, are you?"

"If we can find some sticky saplings," Jeremiah answered.

"Hey, listen to this," Feather called out. "The Bible says that Jacob used poplar *and almond* saplings."

"Almond!" Cody shouted. "We've got almond saplings right out on Eagle Island!"

"Then all we need is a squished bunny," Larry chortled.

"Gross . . . gross . . . gross! You guys can go back out there without me," Feather ranted.

"I thought you might want to come since I have these!" Jeremiah pulled a tool out of his back pocket.

"Needle-nose pliers!" she exclaimed.

"Yeah. Grandpa had them in his fishing tackle box. That way we can pull the note out of that bottle."

"That's not fair," Feather pouted.

"What isn't?" Cody pressed.

"I want to read the note, but I don't want to watch you harm those animals."

"Harm? We can't harm a dead rabbit. And all we're doing to the eagle is feeding it," he tried to explain.

"I'll go . . . but I'll hide my eyes when it comes to feeding bunnies to carnivorous birds."

Larry dribbled over to the center of the tepee and tugged the pliers out of Jeremiah's hands. "You really think this will reach that note?"

"Yep. I hope it's not a riddle like the note we found in my grandad's old rifle."

"It had to be in there a long time for that tree to grow up all around it," Larry surmised.

Feather leaned over and began to unlace her knee-high moccasins. "Not really. The bottle has been there for a long time, but the note could have been slipped in there by anyone over the years."

"No one would have gotten down on their hands and knees and crawled under some almond branches," Larry challenged.

"No one but us!"

Feather tugged off her moccasins, then stood, and tossed them over her shoulder. "Hey, I'm going to the camper to change for the game."

"Yeah," Larry added, "it's about time for the Lewis & Clark Squad to dazzle the crowd with their incredible skill and on-court charisma!"

"What's he talking about?" Jeremiah heckled.

"I think he misses his lucky lasagna," Cody teased.

"You'll all be pleased to know I brought along my lucky brownies!" Larry announced.

Jeremiah licked his lips. "All right, let's eat them!"

Larry shook his head. "I'm saving them for the finals."

"What if we don't make the finals?" Jeremiah inquired.

"Then we'll eat them as a consolation for our loss."

Jeremiah flopped back down on his sleeping bag. "Let me get this straight—if we lose the game, we eat the brownies today. But if we keep winning, we won't eat them until tomorrow afternoon?"

"Correct. But don't even think of throwing the game, Yellowboy!"

"Me? For a measly taste of one of your mother's mouth-watering brownies? Of course not." Jeremiah rolled over and looked at Cody. "Where did he say those brownies were?"

"I'm going to get ready," Feather announced.

"Yeah. Let's go down a little early and watch the end of Eddie's game," Jeremiah proposed.

By the time the boys pulled on their game shorts, tie-dyed T-shirts, and tennies and met Feather at the back of the camper, Eddie Winterhawk was hiking up the hill toward them.

"How'd your game go, Eddie?" Larry called out.

The big boy seemed to stare past them. "Is Honey up here?" he asked.

"No. She went to talk to Danny, remember?" Feather

skipped down the mountainside toward Eddie, leading the others.

Larry scooted up alongside Eddie. "Is your game over?" he pressed.

"Her team's supposed to play right now, and she didn't show up." Eddie pointed toward the Yellowboy tepee. "She's not with you guys?"

"You think something's happened to her?" Cody asked.

"I don't think she'd be late for a game."

"Maybe she forgot. She didn't say anything to me this morning about having a game. I bet she forgot," Feather suggested.

Worry flashed across Eddie's big brown eyes. "Honey isn't the type to forget."

"You guys probably won your game, didn't you?" Larry asked again.

"Have you guys got time to help me look for her?" Eddie asked.

"Actually . . ." Larry bounced his basketball on the hillside, then caught it with two hands as it bounded sideways. "Our game starts in about twenty minutes, and we have to get prepared."

Eddie stared straight at Cody. "What about it, cowboy? Will you help me? Games are running a little late anyway."

"Oh, yeah . . . well, I mean, as long as we get to the court five minutes before game time." Cody glanced at the others.

"Five minutes!" Larry groaned. "We can't possibly get ready in five minutes!"

"There are more important things than basketball," Feather asserted. "Friends in trouble, for instance."

Larry replied in his high, squeaky, nervous voice. "Hey, I agree. Friends are a lot more important. But how do we know she's in trouble? What if Feather is right? What if she just forgot? What if she'd rather be with that Danny than play basketball?"

Jeremiah flipped the ball out of Larry's hand. "Larry's right. That's why we'll search until five minutes before the game. If she hasn't shown up by the time our game is over, we'll help you look for her some more."

"Yeah, we'll probably blow the shirts off the backs of the Browning Bombers in twenty minutes," Larry bragged.

"The Bombers?" Eddie whistled. "I don't think so! Me and Jeremiah will check the crowd at the intertribal council meeting. You three check among the rigs."

"Right. We'll start over at the west and work our way back," Cody suggested.

"I'd sure like to know where she is," Eddie said, his face tense.

Larry stole the basketball back from Jeremiah. "I'd like to know if your team won its game."

"We won."

"Was it close?"

"Not too close," Eddie reported.

"What was the final score?"

"I think it was 22 to 2."

Larry's mouth dropped open. "Yeah, I'd call that not too close."

Cody, Larry, and Feather hiked through the trailers, campers, and tepees.

"Do you know which one is Danny's?" Larry asked.

Cody rubbed the sweat off his forehead. "I know that dark blue Ford pickup is theirs."

Feather plodded ahead of the boys. When they reached the camper door, Larry glanced over at Cody. "What do we do now?"

"I guess we knock and see if anyone's home."

"Go right ahead, partner," Larry prodded. "Me and Feather are right here behind you."

"Yeah . . . thanks." Cody took a deep breath and knocked on the off-white painted aluminum door. "Hello? Anyone home?"

He quickly stepped back. "No one's home. Let's go."

"Try it again," Feather encouraged him.

Cody stepped back to the door. "Hello! Honey, are you in there? Eh . . . Daniel? Is anyone home?"

"What are you guys doing beating on our camper?"

The voice came from higher up the hillside. Daniel Old Horn marched toward them, Honey Del Mateo at his side.

"We were just knocking on your door," Feather reported.

"Why?"

"We were looking for Honey," Larry replied.

"What's up, guys?" Honey asked.

Feather ran up to her. "Have you been crying?"

"No, she hasn't been crying!" Daniel asserted.

"Eddie asked us to help look for you when you didn't

show up for your basketball game. He thought maybe, you know, you were in trouble," Cody declared.

"She's not in trouble!" Daniel snarled.

"My game's not until 1:30. I don't have my watch, but Danny said it was only 1:15."

Larry glanced at his watch. "It's 1:50!"

"Oh . . ." Danny pulled his watch out of his pocket. "I must have looked at it wrong."

"1:50? Oh, man, maybe I can still help them." Honey darted down the hillside.

Feather took two steps after her. "Honey, how'd you get that big scratch on your leg? It's bleeding."

The dark-haired girl hollered back, "I, eh, cut it on a sagebrush."

Cody turned to Daniel. "How did she get that scratch?"

"You heard her. She ran into a sagebrush. You implying something else?"

Larry hopped between Cody and Daniel. "Not at the moment he isn't, because we have a game that will start soon. Come on, Squad, let's get down to the court."

The earlier game was running late, which meant that Honey got to play a few minutes for her team while Larry, Cody, and Feather watched.

"I wish Townie would hurry up," Larry fumed.

"He'll be here," Cody assured him. "We won't start for another ten minutes anyway."

Feather stared across the court at the crowd opposite

them. "We could begin the game without him. I don't see our opponents anyway."

"Yeah, what if they don't show up?" Cody asked.

"Then we win by forfeit. I don't like forfeits," Larry reported. "You don't really get the satisfaction of winning."

"You found her!"

It was Eddie's deep voice behind them. Jeremiah was with him.

"She was with Danny, and he told her the wrong time," Feather said.

Eddie pounded his big, wide right fist into the palm of his left hand. "Why would he do that?"

"We don't know." Larry shrugged. "Anyway, are you set to play, Townie?"

"I'm as ready for them as I'm going to get," he acknowledged.

Larry spun his basketball on the middle finger of his left hand. "Besides, our opponents haven't showed up yet."

"Sure they have," Jeremiah maintained. "They're right over there." He pointed across the dirt court.

"Where?" Cody questioned. "By those big girls?"

Jeremiah glanced up at Eddie, then back at Cody, and shook his head with a wide grin. "Those big girls *are* the Browning Bombers!"

Six

✺

*I*ve never been so embarrassed in my life!" Jeremiah Yellow-boy moaned as he slumped down on his sleeping bag in the middle of the tepee.

Cody handed him a cold Mountain Dew and then plopped down beside him. "I'll have to admit, Townie, you went above and beyond the call of duty."

"Me? It wasn't my idea! I still can't believe Feather did that to me!"

Larry Lewis dribbled his way into the center of the tall canvas tent. "Whoa, Townie took one for the team today! You should receive player-of-the-game award, even if I fired up the winning shot. We are in the semis, boys and girls!"

"Girl," Feather corrected. "We only have one girl on our team. And Townie's ticked at me."

Larry stopped dribbling and rolled the basketball up his arm, across his shoulder, and down his other arm. Then he reversed the process. "Look, we won the game. Psyching out the other team is just part of basketball."

"Psyching out?" Jeremiah protested. "Since when is telling a girl that I really like her and want to buy her a milk shake at the marina called psyching out?"

"She seems like a nice girl," Feather consoled him.

"Nice has nothing to do with it. She outweighs me by fifty pounds!"

Larry leaned his head back and began to balance the basketball on his nose. "Look, I don't see what's the big deal. We were six points back and about to be eliminated by the Browning Bombers. We had to do something. Feather's ploy worked perfectly when she started telling Raelene about how—"

"DeVonne! Raelene was the big one," Feather corrected him.

"Whatever." Larry shrugged. "When she told DeVonne that you were crazy about her, she got distracted enough for me to break in for a couple of jump shots. It's as simple as that."

"Crazy about her! You said I was crazy about her?" Jeremiah choked.

"Of course not. I merely said you were anxious to meet her, and if you didn't get a chance soon, I was worried about what you might go out and do." Feather pulled a thick blue rubberband off her waist-length, light brown ponytail and began to comb her hair.

"What was I going to do? Rob a bank? Kill myself?" Jeremiah sulked. "Which might not be a bad idea."

"Hey, the way I figure it, the team owes Townie one, so why don't we pay for Townie's and Waltina's milk shakes?" Larry proposed.

"DeVonne!" Jeremiah corrected. "Waltina's the one with the tooth missing."

"Whatever," Larry continued. "How about it? Do we pay for his night on the town?"

"Sounds fine to me," Cody agreed.

"I . . . eh, don't really have the money," Feather admitted.

"No problem—me and Larry will cover," Cody offered. "Now when are you going to get the shakes?"

"After the dance competition tonight," Jeremiah mumbled.

"A moonlight romance," Larry teased.

"That's it" Jeremiah fumed. "I'm not going. You can tell her I'm not doing this!"

Feather scooted over behind Jeremiah and began to rub his neck and shoulders. "Come on, Townie, you can do it. I tell you, she is a nice girl. It's only for an hour or so."

"I can't believe I let you talk me into this!" he groaned.

"Hey, let's go grab an eagle feather. That will cheer you up," Cody suggested.

"Not until Townie checks to see if we can get tomorrow morning's game rescheduled," Larry insisted.

Cody began unlacing his tennis shoes. "Well, we'd better get going. We have to get Townie back so he can dance at 7:00 P.M."

"You've got to get me back so I can eat at 6:00 P.M.," he corrected.

"I'll go find Honey," Feather blurted out as she darted out the open doorway.

"I'll gather up Eddie and talk to them about changing the schedule," Jeremiah offered. "Don't you guys say a word about this thing to him."

Larry glanced over at Cody and winked. "What thing?"

"You know perfectly well what thing!" Jeremiah snapped and stalked out of the tepee.

Larry and Cody gathered the supplies they'd need to make the trap and retrieve the note from the bottle. Then they packed it all down to the marina and waited near the rowboat.

Larry stopped dribbling the basketball on the faded wooden dock and pushed his dark glasses to the top of his blond head. "Tell me the truth, Cody—is the powwow about what you expected?"

"Oh, I've seen Townie dance lots of times at powwows close to home. But this is different. I kind of feel more, you know, out of place than I thought I would."

"Yeah, my dad taught at an inner-city basketball clinic one time in Indianapolis. I went with him and felt the same."

Cody pushed his black cowboy hat to the back of his head. "It doesn't hurt us to see things from someone else's point of view."

"That's what I was thinking. I mean, other than Danny, everyone has treated us well." Larry dribbled the ball back and forth between his legs. "Here comes Eddie. Hey, big man, did you see that great win of ours?"

Eddie Winterhawk lumbered up with binoculars hanging on a strap from his neck and his drum propped on his shoulder. "Jeremiah told me about it! I just can't believe DeVonne likes him."

"You know her?"

"Oh, yeah. She was at the wrestling camp I went to last summer."

"She what?" Larry choked.

"Her dad's one of the instructors. She just came along with him. She didn't wrestle, of course."

"Oh . . . yeah," Larry stammered.

"Anyway, it looks like we play each other tomorrow morning."

Larry stopped dribbling and stared across the marina "Eh . . . we're trying to get the time changed."

"That's what Jeremiah said, but I don't think you'll have much luck." He turned to Cody. "You don't play basketball on Sundays?"

"Sunday mornings."

"Your folks won't let you?"

"Actually, it's just something between me and the Lord. I made Him a promise once. I like to keep all my promises."

Big Eddie stared straight into Cody's blue eyes.

Say something, Eddie. I know . . . I know it sounds weird, but it's . . .

"Hey, that's cool!" Eddie finally nodded. "You have to do what's right for you. Jeremiah says you're really serious about that religion stuff."

Lord, help me not to say something dumb. "Yeah, it's important to me. How about you, Eddie? Is faith in God important to you?"

"Now you're getting personal. But I don't guess I think about it as much as I should."

"Nobody thinks about the Lord as much as Cody does!" Larry's voice sounded high and nervous. "Hey, here comes Townie!"

All three boys waited by the boat dock until Jeremiah approached them carrying a large unopened bag of potato chips.

"What did they say?" Larry called out. "Can we change the time of the game?"

Jeremiah stared down at his shoes. "Nah . . . they said it can't be changed."

"What does that mean?" Eddie quizzed. "Are you playing us or not?"

"I can't play, guys. That's all there is to it. I just can't," Cody sighed.

"I guess we'll have to . . . we'll have to talk about it with Feather," Jeremiah replied.

"Here she comes with Honey," Larry observed. "Are you gals ready to shove off? We've got a game tomorrow morning, and Cody isn't playing."

"Did you want us to boycott the game, too?" Feather asked him. "Hey, that sounds cool, doesn't it? I've done a lot of boycotting with my folks."

"I don't make rules for other people," Cody mumbled, his eyes on the dock in front of him. "You guys can do what you think is right for you."

"I've got to play," Larry announced. "My promise is that if I enter a tournament, I finish it. I'd play them single-handed if I had to."

"Are you sure it doesn't matter to you if we play?" Jeremiah asked Cody.

"You're on your own, partner."

"Well, I guess I'll play," Jeremiah decided.

"How about you, Feather?" Larry asked.

"I think we better get out to Eagle Island. It's getting late enough as it is."

"She's right about that," Eddie agreed.

"In other words, you haven't made up your mind?" Larry pressed.

"Maybe . . . maybe not," she replied and climbed into the front of the boat.

They unloaded their supplies in the small clearing in the middle of the tiny island and hiked toward the almond tree on the north bank. Larry palmed the basketball as he hiked along. "How many of those almond suckers do we need to build the trap?"

"I figure we ought to cut them all out," Jeremiah suggested.

Larry led the crew through the thickest part of the pine forest. "It should make the tree healthier. We used to have to prune the sucker growth on our almond tree back home."

"That reminds me of a Bible story," Cody began.

"Everything reminds you of a Bible story," Honey giggled. "You ought to be a preacher someday."

"Me? You've got to be kidding. I'm scared to death to get up in front of crowds."

Jeremiah began to laugh.

"What are you laughing about?" Feather scolded. "Cody would be a good preacher!"

"He does have trouble talking to groups," Jeremiah revealed.

"Townie, don't embarrass me!" Cody pleaded.

"Take his oral report last spring."

Feather bent her fingers back and began cracking her knuckles one at a time. "What was it about?"

"Townie! I'm warning you!"

Jeremiah picked up a small stick and waved it like a sword in front of him. "Canning in the cavern."

"Canning? Cody did a report on canning?" Honey snickered.

"Well, I think it was supposed to be on calving in the canyon. But he was so nervous he said, 'canning in the cavern.'"

Feather commented sympathetically, "Stage fright, huh?"

"Oh, that wasn't the worst thing. One time in the fourth grade, Cody—"

"Yellowboy," Cody hollered, "if you want to live to your thirteenth birthday, choose your words carefully!"

"See, he was supposed to talk about whales, but he—"

"Townie! Remember Miss Wilton!"

"You wouldn't tell them—"

"If you do, I do!" Cody threatened.

"What about Miss Wilton?" Honey asked. "Didn't she teach third grade at Halt Elementary?"

"She retired after Townie got through with her," Cody declared.

"Cody Wayne," Jeremiah hollered through clenched teeth, "I'll shove these needle-nose pliers up your nostrils if you say another word!"

"This I got to hear," Eddie chuckled.

"Truce?" Cody called out to Jeremiah.

"Truce," came the reply.

When they reached the almond tree, all six got down on their hands and knees and peered in at the small glass bottle.

"Who's going to pull out the treasure map?" Feather asked.

"I'll do it," Jeremiah volunteered.

"Let me do it. I'm the one who discovered the first bottle over here," Larry insisted.

"But Cody's the one who found the bottle with the note in it. He should get to read it first," Feather proposed.

Jeremiah waved the others off. "I have the needle-nose pliers. I'll do it."

Eddie plucked the pliers from Jeremiah's hand. "Now I have them!"

Honey put her arm around Feather's shoulder. "These guys are pathetic. We could be here for days. Give us the pliers."

"You?" Eddie hesitated.

"You heard her," Feather demanded. "If you want something done, ask a woman to do it."

"Woman?" Larry mumbled but was silenced by Feather's ego-slaying scorn.

Honey took the pliers from Eddie and squirmed back under the almond tree. "Come on, Feather-girl."

Feather wriggled in next to her.

"You know it has to be important. You don't just leave any old note in a bottle like that. I bet it's a really old note."

"I hope we can read it," Cody added. "If it's very old, it may be faded."

"I think it's more modern—maybe like a drop for a spy ring. That's it! There might be some information leading to classified government documents."

"In Montana?" Eddie questioned.

"Someone went to a lot of trouble, so obviously it's important." Larry sat on his basketball and peered in at the girls. "We might need to turn it over to the FBI."

"Did you get it yet?" Eddie asked.

"Yeah, hurry up," Jeremiah added.

Honey pulled the pliers back from the mouth of the bottle. "Did you ever see these guys so anxious?"

"Yes. I stole their Oreos one time and locked them out of the barn," Feather laughed.

"Look, if you two don't want to—," Larry began.

"I got it!" Honey hollered.

"What's it say?" Townie shouted. "Come on, let me read it!"

"Feather can read it." The two girls stayed under the tree.

Feather began to laugh.

"What is it?" Eddie demanded.

She handed the note to Honey, and both girls began to giggle.

"What is it? Come on, let us see it!" Larry demanded.

"Is it . . . X-rated or something?" Cody inquired.

Both girls continued to laugh.

Feather held up her hand. "Wait!" she choked out. "I'll read it."

"Are you ready for this?" Honey snickered.

"Read the dumb note!" Larry hollered.

"Okay, here it is." Feather took a deep breath and blew the air out with puffed cheeks. "'August 17, 1989.'"

"Hey, it's really old!" Jeremiah blurted out. "Maybe it—"

"She said 1989—not 1889," Cody proclaimed.

Jeremiah shook his head. "1989? Nothing happened in 1989."

"Read the note!" Larry screamed.

Feather bit her lip, nodded her head, let out another chuckle, and then read, "'May the Cubs win the pennant.'"

"What?" Eddie asked.

"What's the note really say?" Larry pleaded.

Feather handed the note back to Honey. "Put it back in the bottle."

"Wait!" Jeremiah hollered. "Let us see that note!"

"You don't believe me?" Feather challenged.

"May we please read the note for ourselves?" Cody requested.

Honey glanced over at Feather and winked. "Give it to Mr. Nice."

The girls crawled out from under the almond tree and handed the note to Cody. He stared at the paper and read, "'May the Cubs win the pennant.'"

"You're kidding me," Eddie groaned.

"It's obviously a code," Larry insisted. "'Cubs win the

pennant. Cubs win the pennant?' What does that really mean?"

Honey brushed off her hands and knees and handed the needle-nose pliers to Eddie. "Why does it have to mean something?"

"Because people don't just stick a note about the Cubs in an old bottle in Montana!" Larry huffed. "I say it's a code, and we need to figure it out."

"I say we've wasted enough time. Let's build the trap," Cody suggested.

"Give me that note. I'll figure it out." Larry took the folded yellowing paper from Cody and slumped down on a rock. "Let me borrow your binoculars, Eddie. I'll use them like a microscope. There has to be something else, and I'm not moving until I find it."

After Jeremiah and Cody cut the almond saplings, the five left Larry on the rock and hiked back to the clearing. Eddie set up his drum while the others worked on peeling the almond saplings and tying them together with twine. They drove the corner sticks into the packed dirt near the center of the clearing.

"This is supposed to work?" Feather asked again.

"Sure," Jeremiah informed her. "Grandpa says you just put the . . ."

He looked over at Cody.

Both boys spoke at the same time. "Bait! We forgot the bait!"

"Oh, man . . . I can't believe this!" Eddy groaned. "We forgot the squished bunny!"

"This is a totally wasted trip," Honey fumed. "No message in the bottle, no bait—what are we doing out here?"

Cody folded his pocketknife and slipped it back into his jeans pocket. "Maybe there's something we can use for bait on this island."

With her hands on her thin hips and her slightly freckled nose in the air, Feather huffed, "I'm not going to search for dead animals."

Eddie brushed dirt off his bare knees and wiped his hands on his black Nike shorts. "She's right. Live ones would be better."

Feather's eyes narrowed, her face taunt. "No way! We are *not* sticking a live bunny in the trap."

"A live mouse?" Jeremiah refused to look at Feather.

"NO!" she exploded.

Honey had her arms folded across her chest, covering her bruise with her hand. "We probably couldn't catch anything even if we found it."

Eddie ran his fingers through his tangled, long black hair. "Me and Cody could row back and try to find something along the highway."

"I don't want to be left out here without a boat." Feather began to pace the clearing. "What if the water got rough, and the boat sank before you get to the marina? Or what if you got run over crossing the highway and were both in comas for months and couldn't tell anyone we were out here? We would be stranded. No shelter. No clothing. There's nothing to eat but pine nuts."

"And wild almonds." Jeremiah's grin revealed perfectly

straight white teeth. "Whoa, this could be serious; we could be forced into cannibalism!"

Cody jammed on his black cowboy hat and waved toward the channel between the island and the shore. "Or you could yell at one of the boaters to come give you a lift."

"Now that's totally boring. It's the kind of answer I'd expect from you, Cody Wayne." Feather turned to Honey. "He has the imagination of a slug, you know."

"We could swim to shore like Grandpa," Jeremiah added.

"No way. Did you feel how cold that water is? If the boat goes," Feather insisted, "all of us go."

"Yeah, that would be best. That way if we don't find any bait, we wouldn't have to row back out here and pick you up," Cody agreed. "You're right about one thing. If a wind whips up and this lake was choppy, it would be a lot tougher rowing a boat."

Honey pulled her stick flute out of its case and blew a couple of soft notes. "I think we ought to try to attract the eagles anyway. Even if we don't get them down to the trap, they might get into the habit of flying over here."

"We could come out here tomorrow after the finals basketball game." Feather held her long braids straight out from her ears and swooped toward the rock fire ring in the center of the clearing.

"Hey, it could be our victory cruise!" Jeremiah proposed.

Eddy set his drum on the rocks and beat a loud roll. "I'd be the only one celebrating."

"Fortunately, Larry's too far away to hear that." Jeremiah grinned.

Feather pranced over by the almond sapling cage and squatted down. "Don't we have any kind of food to put in the trap?"

Jeremiah stared down at his dusty white basketball shoes. "I've got a bag of sour-cream-and-onion potato chips."

"I've got some breath mints," Honey announced.

Eddy dug into his pocket and pulled out a foil-wrapped object. "I've got a piece of Cajun-spiced jerky."

"Jerky?" Feather danced her way over to Eddy. "That's meat, right?"

"Yeah, it's elk jerky," Eddy reported. "But it's kind of hot."

Honey strolled over next to Feather. "Let's bait the trap and try it."

"Bait it with which things?" Jeremiah asked.

Honey giggled as she dropped a Winterfresh breath mint into the center of the trap. "Everything!"

The first eagle appeared seven minutes into the "Eagle Song." It soared effortlessly above the treetops. Eddie beat his drum. Honey played her flute. Jeremiah danced around the fireless rock fire ring. Feather and Cody sat on a log and watched the blue clear Montana sky.

"You know, the only time the sun strikes this little clearing is at noon." Cody pointed to the treetops. "The rest of the day there are shadows from one side or the other."

Feather pulled the keeper off the back of the silver and green earring and rubbed her lobe. "Yeah, it kinda reminds me of New York City. Have you ever been there?"

"No, but I've been to Seattle. How in the world does this remind you of New York?"

"Well, see, the buildings are so tall that some of the streets only get direct sun around noon."

"I'd rather be here than in New York."

"Me, too," she agreed. "But I might have to live there someday. They have a lot of great acting schools."

"You really want to be an actress?" Cody quizzed.

"An actor. If you want to be politically correct, you say actor."

"I don't want to be politically anything."

"Well, when I made that commercial with Bruce Baxter, he said I had an innate ability to act."

"You mean, it was something you were born with?"

"Yes. But I've had a lot of practice."

"You mean, all those plays you've been in?"

She stared down at her knee-length, dark brown suede moccasins. "No, I meant my whole life has been acting."

"What do you mean?"

"Come on, Cody, you know what I'm like. How would you describe me?"

"Your looks?" Cody felt sweat pop out and roll across his forehead.

"No. I mean, if you had to describe my personality, how would you do it?"

"Oh, man . . . this is, eh . . ."

"What's the matter?"

"I'm scared I'm going to say something stupid."

"Just tell me the truth. I don't have anyone around me who tells me the truth."

"Do I have to look you in the eyes?"

"No."

"Are you going to laugh at me?"

"No."

"You're the only girl I've ever known that I can talk to. I mean, really talk to. It's kind of a comfortable feeling when I'm around you."

"Thanks, Cody."

"You're welcome."

"Go on. There must be more you can say."

"Eh . . . no, not really."

"Oh, come on. When you first met me, you thought I was totally weird, right?"

"No," Cody gulped. "Different maybe, but not weird."

"I know what you were thinking."

"What was I thinking?"

"You were thinking that it was weird that I lived in a tepee, didn't have running water or electricity, that I was crazy for being a vegetarian, home-schooled, radical in my political views. You thought I'm anti-government, anti-family, and anti-God, didn't you?"

"Really, I . . . eh, I didn't know what to think. I'd never met anyone like you."

"Well, I'm not that way. But I've been acting that way for so long I don't know if I can change. For thirteen years I tried to act the way I thought my mom and dad wanted me to act."

Cody scratched the back of his shaggy brown head. "I guess most every kid grows up trying to please their mom and dad."

"Yeah, but it's never been what I wanted in my heart. It's all been an act."

"What did you want in your heart, Feather?"

"I always wanted to be just like you, Cody Wayne."

"Like me?"

"Look at you—you've got everything. Your dad loves your mom. My dad's living with a girl only five years older than me! You've got three great brothers. My brother died in Alaska. You've lived in the same house for thirteen years. I've lived in so many places I can't count them. You've got friends like Townie that you've known from day one. I've known you a month, and you're my oldest friend."

"I am?"

"You've got grandparents, cousins . . . and God. I don't know any of my relatives, and I'm supposed to believe that I'm on this planet by genetic accident. You've got everything, Cody Wayne. I've got nothing. But I'll keep on acting like nothing's the matter."

"You're really acting about all that?"

"Yeah, and I'm good at it, too. You know how good at it I am?"

"How good?"

"Right now I have you convinced that I want to go to New York and study acting and become a great actress."

"Actor."

"Yeah. Well, all of that's an act, too," Feather admitted.

Cody stared at the freckles under her eyes. "It is?"

"What I really want to do with my life is someday find a husband who will love only me like crazy all of my life, and live in one house for fifty years, and go to church on Sundays, and do charity work, and sip tea on my upstairs balcony, and raise happy children, and learn to play the piano, and look as pretty as your mom does when I'm forty." Feather rubbed her nose and glanced sheepishly at him. "I've read too many romance novels."

Cody noticed tears trickling down her slightly sunburned cheeks. "Are you all right?"

"Yeah. Sure. I'm fine." She sniffed, then dropped her chin to her chest. "Not really . . . Cody, how come my dad has to live up in Dixie with that girl? Why doesn't he come home to me and Mom? I've prayed and prayed about it. How come God doesn't do something about it?"

Cody stared down at his boots. "I've prayed about it, too, Feather."

"So what are we doing wrong?"

"Maybe nothing. God gives your dad the freedom to make his own decisions."

"So God just sits around hoping my dad will straighten out?"

"I think He does more than that. Maybe He's nudging your dad to make a better decision."

"Well, I wish He'd nudge a little harder."

"They aren't coming down," Townie called out from the circle of rocks.

Cody looked away while Feather wiped her eyes. "How many are there now, Townie?"

"Three. But they haven't even roosted in the trees yet." He looked over at the trap. "I guess they don't like the bait."

"I vote we head back and come again tomorrow," Eddie called out.

"I'll go get Larry," Cody offered.

Feather pointed to the trees on the north side of the clearing. "No need for that. Here he comes, and he's running like a sasquatch is after him."

Crashing through the trees, Larry carried his basketball in one hand and the binoculars in the other. When he reached the clearing, he screamed, "Quick! Everybody in the boat! Hurry! We don't have much time!"

Seven

Cody, Feather, and Larry sat in lawn chairs in the back of the pickup and watched the dance competition in the arena. The long twilight revealed a growing number of clouds stacking up against the Rocky Mountains to the east. The collar of Cody's black sleeveless T-shirt was soaking wet with sweat. The sound of drums rumbled up the hillside.

Larry tossed his basketball from one hand to the other. "I tell you, it was them. I was sitting out there next to that almond tree, looking back at the marina through the binoculars, and the red Dakota pickup pulled in and started hooking up to a trailer that had two jet skis on the back. I even saw a kid in an Orlando Magic cap dribble a ball in the parking lot—*my basketball!*"

"What did he look like?" Feather asked.

"Like a jerk!" Larry jammed the basketball into the palm of his left hand, turned it upside down, and watched the ball fall to the floor of the pickup bed. "I wish we'd gotten there in time. They took off north. No telling how far they went."

"Maybe it's time to call the sheriff's office," Feather suggested.

"Yeah, right." Larry sighed. "Hello, 911, I have an emergency. I think some kid took my basketball at a gas station in Missoula and is traveling somewhere in northwest Montana. Could you set up roadblocks and search every car? . . . Someday, some way I'm going to get even with him."

"I think revenge is overrated," Cody muttered. He stood up to get a better view of the dancing. "Hey, this is Townie's big performance."

Feather positioned herself beside Cody. "He looks happy. It's cool to have something you enjoy doing so much, isn't it?"

"Kind of like me and calf-roping," Cody agreed.

"See," Larry interrupted, "it's not the money. That ball cost me only $24.50 because of my dad's discount, and we've used it a lot. It's the principle of the thing that really ticks me. Revenge? Yeah, that's what I want!"

Cody balanced himself on the spare tire that lay flat on the pickup bed. "How about you, Feather? Which activity do you enjoy and wish it could go on forever?"

Larry tried to dribble the ball in the back of the pickup. "I just don't like having a ball stolen from me—that's the thing."

Feather stepped up on the other side of the tire. "It used to be reading. Before this summer I read about five books a week."

"You haven't given up reading, have you?" Cody bounced on the tire, which jerked wildly, but Feather kept her balance.

Larry's voice increased in volume. "I don't want them to steal it from me on the court or in a service station. Do you guys know anything about Chinese water torture?"

Feather sprang on the tire, and it was Cody's turn to struggle to stay put. "I've only been reading about one book a week lately," she admitted. "Plus the Bible. I told you I've been reading that Bible, didn't I?"

Larry crowded onto the tire between them. "I don't want some kid thinking he stole this ball from Larry Lewis."

Cody stepped down off the tire. "If reading isn't your favorite activity anymore, what is?"

"I'll admit my motive is personal," Larry blabbed. "Obviously, the guy's mentally off. He'll probably plead temporary insanity and beg for life in prison."

Feather stared straight up at the fading sky. "Being with the Squad's my favorite thing. I've never really had a group of kids where I belonged. I've always been 'Weird Feather.'"

Cody leaned forward with his hands on the top of the closed tailgate. "Maybe you never stayed in any one place long enough."

Larry retrieved his basketball and joined the others at the back of the pickup. "I want the guy in the red Dakota to learn a painful lesson—don't mess with Larry B. Lewis!"

Feather turned to Cody. "Usually other kids put me down so much I'm determined to prove them wrong."

Larry scooted in between Feather and Cody, looking at one and then the other. "Are you two listening to me?"

Cody glanced right over the top of Larry. "It's life on the frontier, Feather. Everyone gets to be themselves out here."

She stood on her tiptoes and stared at Cody's eyes. "I think it's Mr. Nice setting the tone for the whole Squad."

The drums ceased, and the crowd grew quiet to listen to the announcer on the public address system. Larry shouted at the top of his voice, "Is anyone listening to me?"

Over the crackle of the loudspeaker came a deep voice, "Well, go ahead, son. What is it you want to say?"

Larry's face turned mashed-potato-white as the basketball tumbled from his hand. "I can't believe this," he mumbled.

"Did you want to say something?" the announcer repeated.

"Eh . . . I think Jeremiah Yellowboy is the best dancer out there!" Larry hollered at the top of his voice.

"Well, son," the announcer continued, "you have a good eye. The judges have awarded the Chief's Trophy to Mr. Jeremiah Yellowboy from Halt, Idaho, representing the Nez Perce Nation."

The crowd cheered as Jeremiah raised the four-foot-tall trophy above his head.

Larry gazed across the arena. "You see the size of that trophy? Maybe I should take up dancing."

"You'll have to get yourself some beaded buckskins," Cody advised.

"You're the wrong color, paleface," Feather teased.

"Oh, yeah, I forgot."

Feather interlaced her fingers and put them on top of her head. "That's what I like about you guys. You forget all about people's differences."

At 9:30 Jeremiah returned with a sheepish smile and several drops of chocolate milk shake on his T-shirt.

"Whoa, the main man returns! How are your adoring fans?" Larry teased.

"He only has one adoring fan—DeVonne," Eddie heckled.

"It wasn't as bad as I thought it was going to be. That's all I have to say about that."

"Someday you'll thank me for setting you up," Feather laughed. "Here, come take my place."

Jeremiah plopped down on the carpeted dirt floor and glanced at the Risk gameboard. "Which color are you?"

"Pink. I've got Australia and Southeast Asia. I've declared them nuclear-free zones and am negotiating a nonaggression pact with Eddie."

"You what?"

"She wants to go to the camper and read," Cody interpreted.

At about 10:30 Larry dozed off to sleep.

At 11:00 Eddie sauntered out into the night to return to his folks' travel trailer.

Cody knew it was close to midnight when he picked up the game and pulled the pillow over his head.

He didn't know if Jeremiah slept at all.

By the time the sun rose above the towering granite peaks of the Rockies, Cody had hiked alone above the sprawling encampment. A brief cloudburst during the night had settled the dust on the dried grass. The air was clean and fresh. With no clouds in the sky, Cody could see for miles in every direction.

Lord, I'm going to let my team down today.

I sure would like it if they really understood why I have to do it this way. You know, Lord, I don't have nearly the self-discipline that they think I have. But if I break one promise to You, the next one will be easier to break. And pretty soon, my promises wouldn't mean anything.

To You.

To anyone.

Cody climbed up on a three-foot-high boulder and gazed down at the gathering of tents, tepees, and trailers. Then he turned and looked west at the Salish Mountains. There were no structures. No roads. No people. For several minutes he gazed out at the wilderness.

This is not a good day. I'm letting my team down, . . . and I have a growing resentment for Danny. This doesn't feel like a Sunday. I wish I could just wake up and be in my bed at home. Sometimes, Lord, I just want to walk away from a situation.

Have You ever felt that way?

Man, I'm glad You didn't walk away!

Feather played aggressive defense.

Larry, as usual, cut and slashed his way to the basket.

Jeremiah looked tired and moved slowly.

And big Eddie led his team to a 14 to 12 lead before Larry called the Squad's first time-out.

"We can do it, you guys. We're in a rut, and they're

starting to figure us out. We've got to try something they won't expect."

Cody drew x's and o's in the dirt. "Larry, why don't you post up at the top of the key, then fake a drive to the basket, and step back and fire up a three."

"I don't shoot threes."

"That's my point," Cody suggested. "They'll give you a clear shot to the basket."

"What if they come out and guard me?"

"Bounce-pass it to Townie; he fakes the long shot and tries for a lay-in."

"I do what?" Jeremiah gasped. "I don't drive, especially on someone like Eddie."

"That's the point. No one will expect it," Cody encouraged.

Larry glanced at Feather and Jeremiah. "Let's try it."

He brought the ball in to the three-point line. Feather set a pick, and Larry used it to start a drive to the basket. She took off to the corner, drawing her man with her, and Larry backed behind the line, leaving his defender to stare as the ball sailed to the hoop.

Nothing but net.

"All right! The cowboy was right!" Larry shouted.

That field goal was followed by one from Eddie. Then the Lewis and Clark Squad repeated the play. This time the other team didn't give Larry much room, but he tossed up his bomb, which banked straight into the net.

Eddie came back with a quick hoop, and the score was tied at 18. Larry called for the Squad's second and last time-out.

"This time let Townie try the head fake and lay-up," Cody urged.

"I'm so tired I could pass out," Jeremiah confessed.

Cody pointed to some kids watching the game from the far side of the court. "I thought maybe that would pep you up."

"One shot for DeVonne," Larry pleaded.

"You could be a game-winning hero," Cody prompted.

"Or I could totally embarrass myself," Jeremiah mumbled.

As Cody expected, the kid guarding Larry played him extra close. He had no chance to shoot a three. Eddie didn't fall for Feather's fake to the corner. Larry bounce-passed the ball to a tightly guarded Jeremiah. Clutching the ball with two hands, he faked a quick shot. The defender left his feet to try and block the shot, and Jeremiah broke to the basket. Eddie lumbered over to block the lane. Jeremiah tried to dribble around his cousin. The ball hit a rock in the dirt and bounced sideways. With his head down, Jeremiah dove to retrieve the ball at the same time as Eddie.

The result of their heads colliding was a noise like a wooden bat hitting a baseball. Eddie staggered. Jeremiah collapsed to the dirt. The basketball rolled out of bounds.

Cody sprinted to Jeremiah's side. By the time he got there, Eddie was helping him to his feet. "Sorry, cousin."

"Everything's kind of blurred," Jeremiah groaned. "I've got to go lay down."

"Put your arm around my shoulder," Cody offered. "I'll help you."

Jeremiah looked over at the kids watching the game. "No. I'll walk off. I'm going up to the tepee and lay down. You've got to finish the game for me, Cody."

Eddie scooted in next to Cody. "The officials want us to finish up the game."

"What about it, cowboy?" Larry urged. "How about you coming in for the last shot?"

Cody felt his chest tighten, and his breathing grew short. "I can't, guys. I just can't!" He felt tears well up in his eyes.

Feather stepped closer to him. "Larry and I can take them on for one shot. Let's try Hoosier #31, Larry."

Expressionless, Larry stared at her . . . then at Cody . . . then at Eddie . . . and back at Feather. "Yeah! You're right!"

Feather tried to inbound the ball to a double-teamed Larry Lewis. Larry broke free for a second and took the pass. He immediately bounce-passed it back to Feather and then broke to the basket.

Only a step in front of the half-court line, Feather took the ball in her right hand and tossed an overhand pass toward Larry.

It wasn't a good throw.

The ball sailed too high.

Way too high.

It hit the backboard, then ripped through the net without touching the rim.

"Yes!" Larry screamed. "Yes . . . yes . . . yes!" He ran over to Feather, grabbed her around the waist, lifted her off her feet, spun her around twice—then turned bright red and released her.

She had a wide grin on her face as the two of them sprinted over to Cody. "Did you see that!"

"That was the greatest non-shot I've ever seen!"

"Hey, guys." Eddie and an older man walked toward them. "Sorry about clobbering Jeremiah. Where is he anyway?" Eddie inquired.

"He went up to the tepee to lay down," Cody reported.

"And we're sorry we had to beat you." Larry grinned. "We were saving our secret weapon for last." He draped his arm over Feather's shoulder.

"Well, here's the thing," Eddie began. "This is Mr. Dollar, who heads the basketball tournament. It wasn't my idea, guys."

"I'm sorry to bring bad news." The dark-skinned man with chiseled features and a shoulder-length gray ponytail spoke up.

"Bad news?" Larry asked.

"Our rules are quite clear. If any team cannot field three people, they must forfeit the game to the other team."

"That's just at the beginning of the game, right?" Larry pressed. "We had three at the start of the game. You've got to be kidding!"

"Sorry, but you're disqualified. Eddie's Eagles move on to the finals."

No one said a word as they hiked back to the tepee. Feather and Larry went in to check on Jeremiah and give him the report. Cody stayed outside.

Lord, I ruined it for the team. All I had to do was enter the game and stand at the back. Maybe I'm taking this too serious.

For several minutes he stood outside the tepee and gazed at the distant mountains.

"Hey, are you coming in or not?" Feather called out.

"I didn't figure you three would be too happy with me."

"Come on, cowboy. This is no time to sulk."

"I wasn't sulking."

"Yes, you were." Feather put her hands on her hips and tilted her head to the side. "To sulk means to brood, mope, and pout. That's exactly what you are doing."

Cody filed into the tent ahead of her and glanced down at Jeremiah lying flat on his back. A bump the size of a half-dollar swelled on his forehead.

"Townie, are you all right?" Cody asked.

"I'll be okay. I hear Feather-girl whipped their tails."

Cody stared at the top of his boots. "We, eh . . . lost the game, Townie."

"Hey," Larry piped up, "we beat them with the bas-ketball. They beat us with the rulebook. Did you see that shot of Feather's? Was that awesome, or what?"

She rummaged through a brown paper sack full of gro-ceries and pulled out a Granny Smith apple. "I told you guys I was just trying to pass to Larry."

"She's just modest and shy," Larry remarked.

She wiped her mouth on the back of her hand. "Never in my entire life have I been accused of being modest and shy!"

Cody sat down cross-legged next to the sprawling

Jeremiah Yellowboy. "I wouldn't blame you if you were all really mad at me."

"Mad?" Larry pranced around bouncing his basketball on the carpet-covered dirt floor of the tepee. "Look at us! Over here we have the pride of the Nez Perce Nation, who loves to dress up in beaded buckskins and dance to drum music. Then we have Feather-girl, who was named by the trees, who thinks she's growing up in the sixties. And you, cowboy, throwing a rope and talking to the Lord like He was standing right there next to you all the time."

"How about you?" Feather challenged.

"Look at me—Larry Bird Lewis. I've got a basketball in my hands twenty-four hours a day. It's an addiction." He dribbled the ball back and forth between his legs.

"Is this going somewhere?" Jeremiah teased.

"Yeah. The point is, the thing I like best about the Lewis and Clark Squad is that nobody tries to change anybody. Did you ever notice that? We can just be ourselves. You guys don't have to be like me." Larry caught the ball and stared at the writing on it. "Nobody on earth has to be like me," he softly confided.

"A philosophical Larry Lewis?" Feather tapped her forehead with the index finger on her right hand. "I like that."

"It was just a temporary lapse," Larry laughed. "Hey, now that we know how far Feather can toss the ball, I just figured out a new play. Oh, man, this will be so cool!"

The wind blew from the northwest and made the waters of Flathead Lake choppier than on their previous trips. Even though the day was clear and warm, the breeze off the water felt cool on Cody's bare arms as he and Eddie rowed across the inlet to Eagle Island.

"We're leavin' at 2:30 no matter what," Eddie insisted. "I've got a championship game at 3:30."

"Ah-hah! Little does he know that the Ft. Hall Hawks have paid us $100,000 to keep him away from the game!"

"A hundred grand?" Eddie laughed. "I'm impressed. I had no idea others recognized my true value!"

"Do you guys really think this will work?" Feather called out from the prow of the boat.

"Well, we didn't find any roadkill, but Larry brought a package of hamburger meat. That should—"

"Eh . . . guys," Larry interrupted, "look, the minimart didn't have any hamburger."

Cody and Eddie both stopped rowing at the same time.

"You told us you had the bait!" Jeremiah roared.

"Oh, I do, I do," Larry insisted. "Only it's not hamburger meat."

"What did you get, Lewis? Twinkies?" Eddie questioned.

"No. I got the next best thing to hamburger. I bought two packages of hot dogs."

"Weenies? You expect us to catch an eagle with cold weenies?" Jeremiah scoffed.

Cody was tying off the boat rope to a rock when he heard Jeremiah holler from the clearing in the middle of Eagle Island. "What's Townie yelling about, Feather?"

"He said, 'We did it!'"

"Did what?"

"Caught something in the trap."

Cody waited for her to lead up the trail.

"You go first. I don't want to see something yucky!"

When he reached the clearing, Eddie and Jeremiah were dancing around the empty trap holding feathers in each hand. Honey and Larry had squatted down next to the almond sapling cage.

"How many feathers?" Cody called out.

"Four! Can you believe it?" Jeremiah shouted.

"I can't believe any eagle would fall for onion-and-sour-cream potato chips."

"I don't think he did. Look at this." Honey pointed toward the trap.

Cody dropped down on his knees beside her.

"The eagle came down after that!" Larry pointed to small furry remains in the middle of the trap. "What do you think it was?"

"This is really gross!" Feather gagged.

"Some varmint came in to get the jerky, and the eagle came after the varmint."

"But the eagle escaped."

"Not without shedding four feathers!"

"Now what are we going to do with these?" Larry motioned toward the two packages he held in his hand.

The last three weenies were still roasting on sticks when a shout from the waters of Eagle Inlet caused them all to jump to their feet and hike to the west side of the island. They stared at two rowboats only fifty feet from the island.

"Danny!" Honey called out. "Danny, what are you guys doing out here?"

"We found a marina rowboat at Eagle Island and decided to take it back where it belongs."

"That's our boat!" Larry protested.

"It's not funny, Danny," Honey yelled. "Bring the boat back!"

"What?"

"She said bring the boat back!" Cody shouted.

"Can't hear you. Have a nice day!"

Larry turned to Jeremiah. "He's kidding, isn't he?"

"They're rowing toward the marina. I don't think they're kidding," Cody groaned.

"He'll come back." Honey's voice cracked. "I think."

"He better come back soon. I've got a game!" Eddie griped.

"I can't believe anyone would do this!" Cody stormed. He picked up a golfball-sized rock and hurled it out into the lake in the direction of the departing rowboats.

Feather shaded her eyes with her hand. "He's not turning around."

Jeremiah sat down on a rock and started pulling off his tennis shoes. "I'll swim over and get our boat back."

"No way. It's too far," Larry warned.

"And too choppy," Feather added.

"My grandpa did it. I can do it."

"Get real, Townie," Honey cautioned. "This isn't a time to take chances."

Jeremiah pulled off his socks, jammed his wallet into his shoes, and then handed them to Feather. His words came slowly and softly. "I need to do it. It's important to me."

"I'm coming with you," Cody announced.

"You guys are nuts," Larry blurted out.

"We swam across Expedition Lake at home. This is not any farther than that," Cody explained.

"I can't believe this!" Honey groaned. "Why are you doing this?"

"It's a family tradition." Jeremiah eased himself slowly into the water. He drew a quick breath. "Man . . . this is cold!"

Cody handed his boots, belt, watch, wallet, and cowboy hat to Feather. "And why are you doing this, cowboy?" she asked him.

"'Cause you got to stick by your friends. And besides, I want to pay back good ol' Danny-boy."

Jeremiah was into the water up to his neck. "The feathers! I want to carry the feathers!"

Cody stepped back out of the water and reached for the feathers.

"All of them?" Eddie called.

"No, just mine," Jeremiah replied. "I want to taste the feather in my mouth while we swim."

"Give me the fourth one," Cody requested. "I might as well do it right."

"I'll be praying!" Feather called as he reentered the water.

So will I, Feather-girl . . . so will I. Lord, I really hope we know what we're doing.

The feathers in their mouths kept both boys' heads up out of the water and prevented any communication. After about ten minutes of swimming, Cody began treading water and waited for Jeremiah. He floated on his back and held the feather in his hand above water. "Townie, are you all right?"

Jeremiah pulled his feather out of his mouth. "Yeah, I guess. But it looks a lot farther when you're on the water, doesn't it?"

"Yep."

"This was kind of stupid, wasn't it?" Jeremiah admitted.

"The water's getting choppier."

"Maybe we should have thought it over a little longer."

"Nah," Cody reasoned, "we would never have tried it if we had thought about it much."

After several more minutes, he heard Jeremiah holler, "Wait up!"

Cody floated on his back.

"Cody, you think we can make it?"

"We've got to."

"Are you scared?"

"Are you, Townie?"

"Yeah."

"Me, too. You know what's funny?"

"At the moment, I could use a good joke."

"When I got in the water, I was so mad at Danny I could hang him from a flag pole."

"And now?"

"Now I just want to make it to shore. The deal with Danny seems really unimportant."

"Yeah, I know what you mean. You ready to start again?"

"Let's do it."

"How about a little slower pace?"

"You lead." Cody motioned with the feather.

Cody figured they had swum for another ten minutes, stopping twice, when Jeremiah waved in the direction of the marina. Cody stared above the horizon of water.

A jet ski? Cody quit swimming and pulled the feather out of his mouth. "Is he going to run us over or rescue us?"

The wake from the jet ski slapped Cody in the face. The kid on the jet ski pushed his goggles to the top of his head. "Hey, are you guys in trouble or just out for a swim?"

Jeremiah gazed at Cody. "I've got to make it all the way on my own, partner."

"I'm not leaving you, Townie. I'd have to spend the rest of my life hearing you brag about how you outswam me."

"Do you guys need some help or not?" the kid hollered.

Cody continued to tread water. "No, we can make it. But there are four kids stranded on Eagle Island out there. Can you get someone at the marina to give them a lift to shore?"

"Sure . . . no sweat."

Jeremiah caught another whitecap in the face, shook

his head, and then glanced at the kid. "Say, you guys don't happen to drive a red Dakota pickup, do you?"

The blond boy's smile widened. "How did you know?"

"Just a guess." Jeremiah jammed the feather back into his mouth and began to swim.

Within a few minutes Cody spotted a water-ski boat skimming out to Eagle Island. When he and Jeremiah were still a couple hundred feet from the shore, the boat returned to the marina. Once the swimmers made it past the buoys that marked off the marina, the water settled down, and they continued in a slow dog paddle.

Both boys crawled on their hands and knees up the muddy shore. Jeremiah flopped on his back. "That was without a doubt the stupidest thing I ever did in my life!" he gasped.

Cody sat on a rock and leaned forward, heaving for air. "How about that time you had a pack of firecrackers in Mrs. Wilton's class?"

"Okay . . . okay, this swim was the second stupidest thing I ever did!"

"But we made it, Townie!"

"Yeah. I've never felt so tired and so good at the same time. I can't wait to tell Grandpa that I swam the inlet with an eagle feather in my mouth!" Jeremiah sat up and looked over at Cody. "Thanks for coming with me, cowboy. It would have been a lot tougher if I hadn't had you along."

"I know what you mean. I kept thinking that if you can do it, I can do it."

"That's what I was thinking about you!"

"We're both crazy."

"Are you still mad enough to hang Daniel?" Jeremiah panted.

"Yeah, but not until I rest up. Let's go find the others."

Jeremiah pointed to the rocks above them. "Looks like they found us." Feather and Larry scampered across the granite boulders to where the two now sat.

"You made it!" Larry shouted. "The iron men of the Lewis and Clark Squad."

"Sometimes it's hard to distinguish between desperation and courage," Cody mumbled.

"Nonetheless, it was heroic," Feather praised them.

"Piece of cake." Jeremiah grinned and then looked over at Cody and shook his head. "Don't ever, ever let me do something that dumb again."

Feather handed the boys back their belongings. Cody tugged his socks on over his wet feet and slipped them into his boots. He stood and tried brushing mud off the knees of his soaking-wet jeans. "Are Honey and Eddie all right?"

"Yeah. Eddie hurried to get ready for the championship game."

"And Honey?"

"She's with Danny."

"Danny? I presume she's going to break his neck for stranding us out there!"

"I don't think so. She likes him, Cody Wayne."

Cody tried wringing water out of his sleeveless T-shirt. "He doesn't seem to treat her very well."

"She says he treats her really nice when he's not

afraid of the competition. She really did get that sagebrush scratch by accident."

"And the bruise?"

"Danny apologized for squeezing her arm too tight. Did you know he brought her a beautiful bouquet of wild-flowers?"

"But he's so . . . so arrogant—or something."

"He's so unlike Cody Wayne Clark!"

Larry carried his basketball and scurried to keep up. "What I want to know is, how did you and Townie get the guy at the marina to come pick us up before you made it to shore?"

"Didn't he tell you about the kid on the jet ski?"

"The what?" Larry croaked.

"The kid in the red Dakota is the one who came out to us and took the message to the marina."

"My autographed basketball! Where is he? I'll—I'll . . ."

Cody and Jeremiah stopped walking. "He did help us."

"Yeah, but . . . okay, I won't hang him. I'll just have him arrested and thrown into the slammer for life."

"Oh," Jeremiah said with a grin, "I thought maybe you were going to propose something drastic."

"You could just forgive him." Cody shrugged. "Anyway, let's go see good old Danny."

"You could forgive him, too." Feather spoke softly.

"That's entirely different!" Cody felt his face warm even though his clothes still dripped cold water.

"Where is that red Dakota anyway?" Larry ranted.

"That one out on the highway headed south toward Polson?" Feather pointed. "It just left the parking lot."

"Ahhh!" Larry hollered. "I can't believe it. I'm going to have nightmares for a year about a red Dakota driving off with my autographed basketball."

"You know what I was thinking?" Jeremiah asked.

"That we should hog-tie Danny and take him out to Eagle Island and feed him to the eagles?" Cody suggested.

"Nope. I was thinking what a great weekend this has been."

"Great? How can you say that?" Larry groaned.

"Look, I won the dance competition, got my very own eagle feather, swam to shore from Eagle Island, will have the naming ceremony tonight, spent the time with my very best friends, and had a milk shake with a, er, nice girl. Hey, it's been a good weekend."

"But you didn't mention losing the tournament, my stolen basketball, and the big knot on your head," Larry reminded him.

"Or getting stranded on Eagle Island," Cody added.

"Slight setbacks—that's all." Townie beamed.

"Hey, here comes Honey . . . and Danny!" Feather pointed across the marina parking lot.

"What's he got in the brown paper sack? His ego?" Larry groused.

"I wish I had my rope," Cody mumbled.

Honey ran ahead of Danny and reached them first. "Before you say anything, Danny wants to apologize!"

"Look, I'm sorry. I was going to come back for you. It

was just a joke," Danny explained. "You didn't have to swim."

"Actually," Jeremiah said, running his hand through his wet butch haircut, "I want to thank you for being a jerk. If it weren't for that, I would never have known I could make that swim."

"You aren't mad at me?" Daniel asked.

"Not when I have this!" He held up his eagle feather.

"You got your eagle feather?"

"Yep. How about you?"

Danny glanced down at his feet. "No. I have to use my stepdad's."

Jeremiah stuck his feather behind his ear. "Say, have you got a bag of Oreos in your rig?"

"Eh . . . yeah." Danny nodded. "Why?"

"We're having a party in our tepee after the naming ceremony tonight. You're in charge of bringing Oreos."

"You really want me to come?"

"Yep. Don't we?" Jeremiah looked back at Cody.

I can't believe this. Lord, this is the part I hate the worst! Just when I really feel justified in hating this guy for life, Townie up and forgives him! You're doing this on purpose, aren't You? Cody cleared his voice with a cough. "Sure. It's a . . . it's your party, Townie."

"Oh, wow! I almost forgot!" Honey bubbled. "Danny has a present for Larry."

"For me?"

Daniel Old Horn reached into the sack and pulled out a basketball. "Think of it as a peace offering. I honestly didn't figure any of you would try to swim ashore."

"My autographed basketball! This is totally incredible!" Larry picked up the basketball and began dribbling, one in each hand. "How did you get it?"

"They were just getting ready to leave when we reached the marina. So I asked him to show me how to drive a jet ski," Honey cooed and batted her eyes. "While he was looking the other way, Danny lifted it out of the back of the rig."

"You stole it from him?" Cody asked.

Danny flashed a half-grin. "I returned it to its rightful owner."

Larry grabbed up the basketballs. "Maybe you're right, Townie! This is a pretty good weekend!"

"Then you guys aren't still mad at me?" Daniel asked.

Lord, You did this to me, didn't You? Why does he have to change? I don't want Danny to be nice. I enjoyed him being a jerk.

"I think he's talking to you, Cody Wayne," Feather prodded.

"Yeah," he mumbled, "it's all right. I forgive you."

Daniel held out his hand to shake. Cody's hand still clutched the eagle feather.

I don't want to do this, Lord.

"Cody Wayne?" Feather badgered.

Okay, Lord. Here goes.

Cody took short breaths and felt his hand shake a little. "Eh, right. Here, Danny, this feather is for you."

"You're kidding me! What's the catch? I don't deserve this!"

"Nope, you don't. But everyone ought to get better than they deserve every once in a while."

It was as if a huge cloud lifted from Cody's head.

When he turned to walk away, he felt Feather's arm slip into his.

Townie's right. Maybe this is a pretty good weekend after all.

For a list of other books by
Stephen Bly
or information regarding speaking engagements
write:
Stephen Bly
Winchester, Idaho 83555